UNEXPECTEDLY YOURS

What Reviewers Say About Toni Logan's Work

Share the Moon

"I enjoyed the group camaraderie and the dynamics between the different women. The setting was interesting, and I liked getting to know about the area. The love story was convincing, and I liked the two main characters. *Share The Moon* is a story of love, friendship and passion, with an unusual couple at its centre."—*Kitty Kat's Book Blog*

"It's sweet and quite well-written... I'll keep an eye out for Logan's future novels."—*Jude in the Stars*

The Marriage Masquerade

"The author puts a reader through the wringer, though, with a fair amount of angst that builds as the story progresses that makes for a great conclusion. ...I found the story to be very uplifting and encouraging on several levels. Combined with the larger than normal angst for a fauxmance, it gave me a lot of feels."—*Lesbian Review*

Writing as Piper Jordan

Hotel Fantasy

"Sensual and sexy... Such and fun novella with loads of potential for you to escape beyond the story itself. I loved the premise and the perspective being shared by both Lexi and Molly's points of view. What is wonderful is how intimate it is. A great read that you can indulge in again and again for a little treat!"—*LESBIreviewed*

Visit us at www.boldstrokesbooks.com

By the Author

Share the Moon

The Marriage Masquerade

Gia's Gems

Perfectly Matched

Unexpectedly Yours

Writing as Piper Jordan:

Hotel Fantasy

Decadence: Exclusive Content

UNEXPECTEDLY YOURS

by

Toni Logan

2023

ISBN 13: 978-1-63679-160-9

This Trade Paperback Original Is Published By
Bold Strokes Books, Inc.
P.O. Box 249
Valley Falls, NY 12185

First Edition: September 2023

CREDITS
Editor: Barbara Ann Wright
Production Design: Susan Ramundo
Cover Design By Tammy Seidick

Acknowledgments

A heartfelt thank you to Rad, Sandy, Ruth, Cindy, and the incredible team at Bold Strokes Books. I am honored and forever grateful to be a part of this amazing family. Thank you.

A very special shoutout to Barbara Ann Wright, editor extraordinaire, for your patience and guidance. I can't thank you enough for all you have taught me.

For my wonderful friends who are always there for me. You guys keep me grounded and smiling. I love you.

And finally, to *you*, the reader, for taking a chance on this book. I hope you enjoy reading it as much as I enjoyed writing it.

Chapter One

"What's this?" Allie Aukai sat at the small kitchen table, sipping coffee as she stared at the folded piece of paper her eighty-two-year-old mom had floated in front of her.

"Just read it. And before you come up with a thousand excuses why you can't do it…" Her mother shook a quivering finger at her. "Just remember, it's your father's dying wish."

"Dad's dying wish?" Allie snorted. The only thing she remembered her dad mentioning after the doctor had informed them that he had an inoperable tumor and less than three months to live was that he wished he had learned how to play golf. That was odd. Not because he had always criticized the sport as *unappealing and ridiculous*, but because he was never one to openly talk about regrets. Then again, he never really talked about anything. To Allie, he was a stoic man who'd displayed few words and even fewer feelings, and even though her heart ached from the grief of his recent passing, she was not going to miss his scathing grunts and judgmental facial expressions. If a picture was worth a thousand words, then one of her father's unflinching and unapproving stares was worth double that.

Allie raised a questioning brow. "Does this have anything to do with golf?"

"What are you talking about? Your father hated golf."

"I know. That's what I always thought too, but apparently, I didn't know him as well as I thought I did."

"Just read the note." Her mom waved a dismissive hand.

Allie took another sip, leisurely unfolded the piece of paper and wondered what the father she'd never had a meaningful conversation with had to say to her postmortem. As she glanced over the barely legible cursive that she had come to associate with his arthritic style, a knot began forming in her stomach. "Wait." She choked on the recently sipped coffee. "This can't be right." She glanced at her mom. "*This* is dad's dying wish? Seriously?"

Her mom nodded.

"Well…I'm not doing it." She tossed the paper back on the table. "It's stupid."

Her mom folded her thin, age-spotted arms across her chest and leaned back in her chair. "I told him you'd say that."

"Oh, come on, Mom, are you honestly going to sit there and tell me that you don't think that's a bit crazy?" She gave a nod to the paper. "Was Dad even in his right mind when he wrote it?"

"Your father's state of mind has always been debatable, but…" She pushed the note back toward Allie. "The point is, you know how obsessed he was about that ancient legend."

"Yeah, well, you and I both know that story's a complete fairy tale. Good for telling around a campfire and nothing more. Not something to make a dying wish on."

"I agree. But." Her mom exhaled a heavy breath. "It's his wish, so what am I supposed to do, hmm? Deny him this last request?"

"Yes, because it's stupid and based on something that never happened," she retorted as the memories of a tale that he'd recited to her more than any children's book or nursery rhyme raced through her mind:

"According to the legend of our people," her father began as he sat by the side of her bed in the glow of a night-light, painting a picture that was so vivid and enchanting, she leaned against her headboard, knees tucked into her chest, wide-eyed and glued to every word.

"Our ancestors were peaceful Polynesian islanders who lived in harmony with the sea and land for hundreds of years. When the early explorers showed up, they began trading food and other goods, and for many years, the exchanges worked well for both parties. Until one night, a mysterious ship set anchor off the island, and in the shadow of the new moon, a group of men silently rowed ashore not with the intent to trade but to seize the land and its resources for their own gain." He lowered his voice to emphasize the drama.

"All the islanders who were not killed were taken prisoner. But unbeknownst to the invaders, a handful of men in two canoes had been out fishing all day, and when they returned that evening and saw what had taken place, grief and anger overwhelmed them. They paddled out to the ship, snuck aboard, and attacked the unsuspecting men."

Allie always jumped on her bed during this scene, stabbed at the air with her imaginary sword, and threw in a karate kick or two for good measure.

"They fought bravely to try to free their people, and at one point, it looked like they were gaining the upper hand, but sadly"—he continued in a softer voice—"their spears were no match for the weapons of the explorers. In the end, they lost their lives. Their bodies were dumped overboard, and their canoes sunk. In one night, a beautiful way of life was forever lost."

He grabbed his necklace and cupped his hand over a pendant of a sea turtle that his father had carved out of a shell as a tribute to their people. "But those who survived told the tale to their children and their children's children. Just like I'm doing to you because the blood of an amazing people runs in our veins. Our people." He scooped her up, tucked her under the covers, and gave her a good night kiss on her forehead. "Were good people. And in the end, they fought heroically for what was taken from them. *Never* let anyone take what is rightfully yours."

The stories remained Allie's fondest memories of her father. Before her adolescence, when the whiskey robbed her of his attention, and bitterness permanently dimmed the spark that had once glistened in his eyes. In her teens, her relationship with him was already distant and strained, and by the time she was in high school, they were like two ships passing in the night.

In a last-ditch effort to reconnect with him, she splurged on an ancestry test kit, hoping the results would reignite the bond they'd once shared over the story of their people. But eight weeks later, she'd sat in stunned disbelief as she'd stared at a colorful pie chart that contradicted nearly everything she'd believed about who she was.

From her mom's side of the family, she was part African and French, so that piece of the pie was expected, but Brazilian with a sprinkle of Spanish and German? Really? Where the hell was the Polynesian DNA?

Her mom acknowledged that she had always suspected the story of the island tribe was no more than a fabrication.

"Then, why didn't you say something?" Allie huffed in a disappointed tone as she flopped on the couch while trying to wrap her mind around her new genetic reality.

"Because it's not like I could completely disprove the claims. But, honey, I'm telling ya, if ever there was a group of people who would benefit from taking some form of antipsychotic medication, your father's side of the family is it." She chuckled as she sat with Allie. "It's kinda fitting your grandfather died jumping off a cliff. That man was batshit crazy, and there are times I really wonder how much of it rubbed off on your father."

"Huh. Well, that explains a few things." Like her mom's not so subtle eye rolls or well-placed snorts every time her dad would talk about her grandpa.

"And my advice to you is, don't be sharing any of those results with your father. You need to keep this between us, Allie."

"But don't you think he would want to know who we really are?"

"No. I'm telling you, just leave it be."

"But not telling him just perpetuates the lie."

"Listen to me, Allie. That damn legend makes your father think there's something special about him that stands out from everyone else. Believing he's a descendant of a small tribe of people who took on a ship full of armed men with fishing spears makes him feel proud. So don't go popping that bubble, okay? Instead, just do what I've done all these years."

"Which is?"

"Nod, smile, and say, yes, dear, every time he brings up anything about his family. Trust me, you'll understand when you're in a relationship of your own how those words can add years to a marriage."

"But—"

Her mom held up her hand and exhaled a heavy sigh. "Look, if you end up telling him, he'll just get angry and deny it, and I think it would be in the best interest for both of us if we don't upset that apple cart, if you know what I mean."

Allie knew exactly what she meant. News like that would definitely put him in a rage, send him reaching for the bottle, and shortly thereafter, the whiskey demon would emerge, and that was never a good thing.

"Besides." Her mom flashed a smile and patted Allie's thigh. "I'd rather have him believing in that damn story than believing he can fly off a cliff."

Allie nodded. True. Of the two, at least believing in the legend wasn't going to end in bodily harm. *So with a heavy sigh and a promise to her mom, she deleted the evidence of her true ancestry and mastered the art of smiling and nodding.*

"Anyway." Her mom's soft voice brought her back to the present. "Getting back to his request." She pointed at the note.

Allie refocused her attention on the small, crinkled single sheet of paper. Handwritten in a total of two paragraphs were instructions to take his urn of ashes to the coordinates written at the bottom of the note that marked the "valiant last stand" so he could be reunited with his people. He emphasized that he did not want his ashes to be scattered on the surface of the water but buried at the bottom of the ocean at that exact location.

"Ma, where did these coordinates come from?" Not once in the retelling of the legend had he ever mentioned an exact location. She cocked her head in thought. Although, there was that one time he'd mumbled something about Papua New Guinea and the Solomon Sea, but by then, she had smiling and nodding down to a science, and with it came the art of tuning him out.

Her mom averted her eyes as she fidgeted in her seat and fumbled with her coffee cup.

"Ma? What aren't you telling me? Where did dad get these numbers?"

She scoffed. "Oh, all right. He had a dream where one of his ancestors appeared to him and gave him those numbers. When he woke up, he wrote them down and swore they were the coordinates of the battle."

Allie threw her head back in laughter. "You've got to be shitting me. You do realize how insane this whole thing is? Right? How absolutely—"

"I know, Allie, I know. But again, it's his dying wish." She took a moment to take another sip of coffee as they locked eyes. "And don't you give me that look, young lady."

"What?"

"Don't *what* me. I can see your wheels spinning."

Allie leaned forward and shook her head. "I can't believe you're actually defending this. Who cares if it's his dying wish? You want to know how many wishes I've made that have never been answered? Or how about you, Mom. How many times did you openly wish Dad would stop drinking? And how many times did he grant that wish?"

"You have to understand, your father was a different person when we first married, settled into this house, and opened the diner. He was a happy man, full of hopes and dreams." She paused as her expression turned blank, and the lines that were a testament to a life of hard days and long hours deepened into her light brown face. She tucked a loose strand of thinning silver bobbed hair behind one ear, as her chestnut eyes seemingly danced with memories. "For years, we worked nonstop, and every penny we earned, he insisted we put back into the restaurant. A deposit for a payoff down the road, he would say to me. But after decades of struggles, I begged him to sell the place. But your father wouldn't hear of it. He was a proud man, and he kept assuring me that the restaurant would catch on and a nicer car and larger house"—she referenced her meager surroundings—"were right around the corner. You'll see, he would always tell me. But none of that ever happened, and resentment and anger set in, and that's when the drinking followed." She paused. "He always wanted more, Allie. More for himself, more for me." She turned to her. "More for you."

In that moment, with those words still lingering in the air, Allie felt for the first time in her adult life that there was something about her dad that she could finally relate to. Seemed as though she wasn't the only one who had their hopes and dreams for a better future smashed into oblivion.

She had been born an *oops baby* during a time in her parents' lives when they'd mistakenly thought her mom was well beyond her reproductive years. And since babysitters and day care were unaffordable options, she was raised at the diner with the help of other employees and regular clientele who'd gladly watched over and entertained her as her parents worked.

The moment she was old enough to balance food on a tray and scrub dishes, her parents had put her to work, and it didn't take long before she'd realized the restaurant life was not the life she wanted for herself. She had dreams of becoming a journalist, but when serious health complications had struck her father at the start of her high school senior year, she'd made the painful decision to put her future plans on hold, care for her parents, and take a more active role in running the family business.

Resentment? Yeah, she was intimate with that emotion.

Her mom tapped the bottom of the paper. "He wants to be buried here. Those are the numbers he had tattooed on his chest when he forgot where he put the damn piece of paper that he had written the coordinates on. We about tore up this entire house looking for it." She chuckled as she shook her head. "When we found it, he took it upon himself to get the numbers inked on his chest because he knew his lack of memory was becoming more than just senior moments. Losing that paper scared him, and he thought if it happened again, he would lose a part of who he was."

"Wait, back up, Dad got a tattoo on his chest?"

"He did, and don't get me started about that. You'd think he could have gotten something sweet or sentimental, but *no*." She stretched out the last word and laced it with so much disgust, it left no doubt about her feelings.

"Huh." Allie leaned back in her chair and scoffed at the hypocrisy. "And he jumped all over me the day he saw my Pegasus tattoo." Her dad might have been meek in stature, but the verbal assault he could unleash wielded a powerful sting. Twice he had unloaded that force on her. The first time was when he'd seen the colorful ink wrapping around her right forearm, the second was when she'd introduced him to her first girlfriend.

"Your father always thought tattoos on women made them look cheap."

"Oh my God, Mom, you do realize how sexist that statement is?"

Her mom held up a defensive hand. "I'm not taking his side. I'm just telling you what he thought. Now." She gestured again to the note. "Let's give him in his death the one thing that will finally give his soul some peace and happiness. This isn't about DNA or whether the legend is real. This is about a story that he held in his heart for all these years. It became *his* identity, so let it be his final reality. So I'm asking you." She reached over and gently padded Allie's hand. "Please give him this last wish so we can get on with our lives. And if you can't find it in your heart to do it for him, then do it for me. As a favor. Please."

Another rebuttal was forming on Allie's lips as she glanced into her mom's pleading eyes. But instead, she hunched her shoulders in surrender as she turned the paper around and focused on the series of numbers and symbols. She grabbed her phone and typed them into a longitude and latitude app. Within seconds, the phone pinged the location, a red dot pulsing in the middle of a blob of blue.

She flicked the screen, widened it out, and scoffed. "Ma, this is in the Bahamas. That's…" She did a quick Google search. "Almost nine-thousand miles away from Papua New Guinea."

"The Bahamas, huh, well, whaddaya know. Come to think of it, we did watch a TV show on the Bahamas the night he had that dream. But double-check the numbers just in case."

"That's a four, isn't it?" Allie tapped the paper.

Her mom pulled the note closer, bent forward, and squinted. "Yep, that's a four."

Allie reentered the coordinates, and the red dot appeared in the exact location as before. "Yeah, it's the same place. Guess ancestors that visit in dreams shouldn't be trusted with coordinates." Allie giggled with a hint of sarcastic humor that her mom didn't seem to appreciate. After a moment, she cleared her throat, folded her arms, and pushed herself deeper into the back cushion of the chair. "So what do we do now?"

"We do exactly as he wished. If that's where he wants to be buried, then that's where we'll bury him. Whether it's in the Solomon Sea, the Mohave Desert, someone's backyard, or the Bahamas, it doesn't matter. If he took the time to get those coordinates tattooed on his chest, then that's where he'll end up."

Allie took a moment to roll her eyes. Why couldn't his death have just ended with his cremation? Why did he have to add this extra layer of complication to the mix? "Okay, Mom, answer me this: say I agree to this whole thing, which I'm not, but say I do. How are we going to get the money? Huh? You know what a trip to the Bahamas costs? A lot. And neither of us has a couple grand just lying around burning a hole in our pockets."

"Your father asked that some of his life insurance money go toward the expense."

"What? Ma, no. We need that money for the restaurant and house repairs. It's dumb to take that cash and put it toward this." And not only that, but it was also a selfish last act on her father's part, him knowing they could use those funds for so many other things.

Her mom reached across the table, and gently squeezed her forearm. "I may not agree with it, and God knows I could sure use the money, but I don't want the guilt of not doing this weighing on my conscious the rest of my life," she said.

"Mom..."

"I'll be fine." She waved. "And so will the restaurant. We'll figure out a way, we always do. Besides, now that you're running the place instead of your father, I have faith."

Faith, Allie thought, was not going to be the salvation of the restaurant. What they needed was a full-blown miracle to resuscitate the place. And since the chances of that happening were zero to none, last week, she'd begun the process of trying to convince her mom to sell the diner, take what little money she could get for it, and finally retire. Especially since the rent was rising, and their customer base was dwindling. But her mom had refused to even consider it. What was left of their regular clientele she regarded as family, and she had grown to love the place. Allie came to realize that to her mom, the diner wasn't just a business, it was more of a home than the one she lived in.

"When am I supposed to do this?"

"The check was in yesterday's mail. Research what you need and how much it'll cost, and let's get your father where he wants to be."

Allie reluctantly nodded as she glanced around for the urn that, up until now, had been on the mantle over the fireplace, bookended by framed family photos. "Where's Dad? Did you move him?"

"He's in the liquor cabinet." She motioned with a tilt of her head. "I decided to put him in there because it just seemed like a more appropriate spot for him."

Allie shuffled over to the cabinet and opened it. Sure enough, her father's urn was sitting next to a half-empty bottle of his favorite whiskey. She smiled and shook her head at the remains of someone who was more a boss to her than a dad. It was the perfect place for a father whose two greatest loves in his life were the restaurant and booze.

"He was still your dad." Her mom appeared by her side, reached over, and removed the corded necklace of the sea turtle that was wrapped around the neck of the urn and placed it over Allie's head. "I know he was not the best father, but he loved you very much." She patted the shell pendant against Allie's chest.

Allie sighed as feelings of obligation, more than sentiment, kicked in. Not so much for her father but for her mother. It was clear that fulfilling his last wish was important to her. She glanced again in the watery eyes that seemed to be pleading. "Okay, Mom." She surrendered as her mother leaned into her shoulder. Allie placed a protective arm around her mom's small frame and hunched back; she had sacrificed a lifetime for this man. "I'll do it. Just give me some time to do some research and line up how I'm supposed to make this all happen. Okay?"

"You'll make your father's soul very happy."

Allie nodded. She'd given up trying to make his living soul happy many years ago, when she'd realized that nothing she did translated into approval or loving affection. Maybe now, in his death, she could make one last attempt to bring them together.

CHAPTER TWO

Y ou know, I never tire of this view." Kate Williams stared at the ocean from the oversized padded chaise lounge on the equally oversized patio of her gracious beach home that was nestled in a hill on her eighty-acre private tropical cay in the Bahamas.

"This has always been my favorite spot of the whole house."

Brooke's voice floated in Kate's head. She flopped her head to her side and smiled at the image of a curvy redhead, with a splash of freckles spotting her fair skin, lounging on the chair beside her.

"I remember. I also remember the time we made love out here under the stars on that exact chair." Kate tilted her chin toward Brooke.

"You only remember the one time?"

Kate laughed. "Well, one in particular is definitely on my mind right now."

"Hmm." Brooke swung her legs to the floor, faced Kate, and extended her arms. "In that case, I think it's time we—"

"Knock, knock."

Kate startled for a moment, then called to the familiar voice. "I'm on the back porch."

"I should have figured you'd be here." Carla—tall, bronzed, and wearing a floral sundress and flip-flops—settled into the chair that moments ago held a conjured image of Brooke and grabbed the glass of lemonade Kate had placed on the small table between them.

"How are we looking for this week?" Kate returned her focus to the ocean as lingering thoughts of Brooke danced in her head.

"Not bad. Four of the six casitas are booked. Here's the itinerary and info of the guests."

"Thanks, Carla," Kate said in a faraway voice as papers were placed on the table.

A moment of comfortable silence settled between them as Carla whipped out her phone and started flicking at the screen. "You going paddleboarding today?" she asked without looking up.

Kate turned to her. "No, I think I'll snorkel instead. It's been a while since I've been out."

Carla nodded. "Well, next time you want to go boarding, hit me up. You know my schedule."

Kate smiled. "That I do."

They sat for another moment, Kate lost in her own thoughts, before Carla tipped her glass, finished her drink in three gulps, and rolled out of the lounge chair. "Okay, I'm going to head back. Let me know if you need anything else."

"I will. Thanks again, Carla."

"Sure thing, boss."

And with those words and the soft pitter-patter of feet, Carla vanished. Kate glanced at the small stack of papers and frowned. Only four of the six casitas were booked. This time two years ago, there had been a waiting list for people wanting to come to the resort. But times were a little tough, and disposable income was becoming more and more of an issue for most people these days. She thought again about lowering the prices of the add-ons that guests could book during their weekly stay, but she was hovering close to a zero profit margin as it was. If things became worse, she would have to operate at a deficit and tap her own funds to keep the women-only resort going and her crew paid. Hopefully, it wouldn't come to that.

She picked up the stack of papers and read the printouts. Casita One was a couple from London on their honeymoon. They'd booked paddleboarding lessons, snorkeling excursions, morning beach yoga classes, and a sunrise hike around the south side of the island.

Casitas Two and Three were reserved for five women from Canada. Pretty much everything the resort offered in the way of activities and excursions was packed in their itinerary.

Then, there was Casita Four. "Hmm," Kate muttered as she turned over the paper. No excursions or activities. Not that it was rare. Many couples came to the island and wanted to do their own thing, relax on the beach, or focus on romance. But Allie Aukai had booked as a single guest, and in the comments section, Carla had listed that she would be arriving in her own boat. That was troubling. Kate's anxiety kicked up a notch. Shortly after she'd moved to the island, photos had appeared in a tabloid, obviously taken from an offshore boat, of her walking on the beach and lounging on her patio.

"Damn." She began rubbing her temples. They'd left her alone for almost ten years, so why now? The only thing that made sense was that someone wanted to dig up her past and write one of those "where is she now" articles.

She grabbed her phone. "Carla, what's the story on the woman in Casita Four? Any chance she could be paparazzi or press? I'm more than a little suspicious since she's coming over on her own boat."

"She's not paparazzi or press," Carla reassured her. "She's a recreational diver," she said as Kate heard the tapping of keyboard keys. "She sent a copy of her PADI certification last week when she booked her stay, and because she's renting a private dive boat in Nassau, she declined the complimentary ride over."

"A diver? Who approved that?" Kate snapped. When it came to the guests, she liked everyone to stay on script as much as possible and not deviate from the resort's supervised activities or excursions. It allowed for more predictability and limited liability. If someone wanted more than what they had to offer, why not stay at Paradise Island? Why come here?

"What do you mean? I run everything by you regarding the guests' requests, so who do you think approved it?"

Kate pinched the bridge of her nose as she let out a long breath. *Note to self, on the days when I'm in a mental fog, I should not make any decisions regarding the guests or the resort.* "Sorry, Carla, that tone wasn't meant toward you. It must have been an off day because I don't remember approving it. I'm sure everything will be just fine." She had been doing so well lately. The days of feeling like a zombie from existing in an insomnia-induced brain haze were pretty much behind her. But there were always those days, even weeks, when she felt herself slipping backward, her grip on reality tenuous at best. Would she ever be her old self again? Hell, how could she?

"That's okay, boss."

"Well, no, it's not, but thank you." Kate heard someone call Carla's name in the background.

"Anything else? If not, I should probably get going."

"No, go be the amazing person you are. We'll talk later." Kate disconnected the call, tossed her phone on the table, and took a deep breath. This time of the year was always hard. She brought her legs up, hugged them close to her chest, and rocked a bit. It was the fifth anniversary of Brooke's death, and although the shattered pieces of her heart felt haphazardly glued back together, the cracks remained. And they were deep and scarring.

She glanced over at the highest part of her cay and squinted when the sun reflected off a huge bronze sculpture of a bird taking flight. She cupped the pendant of the same image and brought it from around her neck and kissed it. "Miss you, my love," she whispered before letting it fall back to her chest and returned her gaze to the ocean as she let the hypnotic ebb and flow of the waves cause memories to resurface:

Kate had been born Suzanne Bennett, only child and heir to the Bennett family fortune that consisted of an impressive portfolio of national grocery stores, minimarts, and strip mall real estate. But while growing up rich came with its perks, it also came with a high price. While her dad was traveling the globe and—according to her mother—screwing every woman under the sun, her mom was a recurring long-term guest at one of Los Angeles's top celebrity rehab centers. Because of that, Kate was handed off to a revolving door of nannies. And as well-intentioned as some of them were, none had stuck around long enough to be a good role model or parent figure in her life.

Family was a word she had no true reference for, and the few fleeting moments that her parents had just happened to be home at the same time had created tension not unity.

By the time she was eight, she had been whisked away to private boarding school, and when she hit her upper teens, she was already following in their footsteps. A revolving door of women, recreational drugs, and alcohol had rounded out her lifestyle, and it didn't take long before the tabloids caught wind of it all. Pictures of her troubled life were splashed all over their front pages with scandal-ridden headlines. They'd dubbed her *Bad Girl Bennett*, and she became just another spoiled and pathetic rich kid for the public to shake their heads at and *tsk* over.

By the time she was in her twenties, she was emotionally checked out, numb from substance abuse, and bouncing from one Hollywood actress to another. When she'd turned thirty, she'd made a half-hearted attempt to clean up her life after she'd seen an article in one of the tabloids that portrayed her as no more than a go-nowhere, do-nothing, trust fund multi-millionaire living off her family's billion-dollar empire.

Ha, she'd vowed to show them. But her attempt at navigating the world through a sober mind had lasted a grand total of two weeks and one day. But hey, at least she'd tried.

That had all changed one night when she was pulled over for weaving down Sunset Boulevard in her brand-new Beamer and slapped with a third DUI that should have landed her behind bars. But the Bennett family team of lawyers had convinced the judge to swap cell hours for community hours. Her driver's license was suspended, and she was ordered to attend a year of substance abuse counseling. A caseworker was assigned to watch over her progress and reassure the judge that she was indeed following the stipulations in the agreement. After a full-blown tantrum and an empty threat to sue the county of Los Angeles, she'd reluctantly agreed to the demands because the alternative was not an option.

The day Brooke had stepped into her life as the social worker assigned to her case was the day her life had finally turned around. It wasn't the hours of community service or the group counseling that had made a difference. It was having someone ten years her senior believe in her. Someone who'd seemed to genuinely care about who she was as a person instead of her last name. Brooke was a kind, gentle soul who'd made her feel, for the first time in her life, that she was "seen."

They had hit it off from their introduction, and on the dark days when the demons had come calling and Kate had struggled to stay sober, Brooke was by her side offering encouragement and guidance. Eventually, Brooke had persuaded her to stay away from the clubs and decline the celebrity party invitations. She'd ushered Kate into a world of healthy eating, detox, and exercise. The paparazzi and press eventually got tired of the new and boring Suzanne Bennett and shifted their attention to other more sensationalized stories, and in the land of limelight, there were plenty of messed-up celebrities that were worth their time.

By the end of that next year, Kate was yesterday's news to a public whose attention span was about as short as a gnat's and whose ever-increasing appetite for the latest celebrity gossip and scandals was insatiable. On the third anniversary of her sobriety, she'd legally changed her name to Kate Williams and asked Brooke to marry her, hoping the new identity would also give her a new life.

To keep the wedding off the radar and out of the public eye, no one was invited to the ceremony except a minister. When she'd finally broken the news to her parents, they'd seemed genuinely happy for her, or was the emotion she'd felt from them more of relief? When they'd told her they wanted to give her something as a wedding gift, she'd asked for the family's cay in the Bahamas so she could make it her permeant residence. They'd gladly transferred the deed to the house and land into her name.

It wasn't long after she and Brooke had settled there that Brooke began floating the idea of turning the south portion of the island into an all-women resort. She'd thought it would be a great way to provide jobs for some of the lesbian homeless youth she had once worked with over a decade ago and still maintained close friendships with. At first, Kate was extremely reluctant to bring anyone to the cay, much less a group of full-time employees who would live on the island with them. She was tired of people and was enjoying a life of solitude.

But Brooke was just the opposite. She'd thrived on being social, loved people, and couldn't help but want to give back to the community in some way. "They just want what you've had since birth, an opportunity for a better life," she'd told her. And because Kate loved Brooke unconditionally, she'd of course said yes.

As the months passed, Kate had relished watching Brooke glow when she'd talked about designing the resort and the opportunities the place would provide to those she knew needed a job and a safe place to live. They'd hired an architect out of Miami to design six guest casitas that would face the ocean and follow the curved shoreline of the cay. Each would be an eight-hundred-square-foot, one-bedroom suite with a living room, small breakfast nook with minikitchen, and a pull-out sleeper sofa to accommodate a maximum capacity of four for the more budget conscious groups.

Cabins had been built up the path from the casitas for twelve full-time staff members, a physician, a chef, and two groundskeepers. They also had the architect design a commercial kitchen and open dining area that would be built close to the lagoon, and a hut just off the dock that would provide free drinks and snacks from dusk till dawn. Golf carts would be the mode of transportation around the island, and they'd decided on concrete instead of natural paths for easier access around the grounds.

It took over two years to complete Brooke's dream, and when it was finished, they'd christened the resort Rainbow's End as a symbol of new beginnings. Life was good, and Kate had felt as though she finally had a purpose and someone who truly loved her by her side.

Then, the unthinkable happened on an evening walk to the top of the hill to overlook the sunset. Brooke had collapsed.

The rest of the memory was blurry pieces strung together. There had been a medical helicopter, the bright lights of the hospital, and people shoving themselves in her personal space as they'd asked a barrage of questions. She remembered holding Brooke's hand and telling her she loved her before they wheeled her away for surgery, and that all would be okay. Then came the waiting, the pacing, and the endless glances at a clock that seemed to defy time until a figure had walked up to her, peeled his scrub cap off, and said things to her that her brain couldn't comprehend. The room had begun spinning, and as much as she'd tried to focus on the doctors' words, nothing was making sense. An unknown birth defect in Brooke's heart valve, a long medical name she couldn't understand, much less pronounce, and then the words that had caused her to tumble to the floor in a ball of pain: "I'm sorry. We did everything we could."

For the next several months, she'd stayed in her house, not engaging with anyone. Phone calls and text messages went unanswered. Her weight plummeted and so did her outlook on life. Carla had taken over running the resort, and every morning and evening, she left a tray of food on Kate's back patio table that, more times than not, was left untouched. And even though Carla knew Kate had made a promise to Brooke to never drink alcohol again, she'd still ordered all the resort's liquor to be locked up after the guests went to bed, knowing Kate would probably want to wrap herself in a blanket of familiar numbness.

As temping as it was, Kate had never broken her promise.

It took a year before the statue had arrived, and she'd thought the bird lifting off the ground in flight was the perfect tribute to Brooke's spirit. On the evening Kate had taken her ashes to the top of the hill, she'd waited until the last ray of light had glistened off the tip of the bird's one wing before spreading Brooke's ashes around the base.

"Fly free, my love," she had whispered as she'd choked back the tears. A moment later, a sudden guest of wind had picked up, and just like that, Brooke had become one with the sky, the sunset, and the ocean. And as Kate had returned to her house, something had lifted inside her as an inner voice of Brooke had told her that everything was going to be okay, that *she* was going to be okay.

A low grunting sound brought Kate back to reality. Gizmo, her brown and black pet pig—who'd washed ashore exhausted and barely alive the day after she'd spread Brooke's ashes—addressed her with a customary greeting.

"Good morning, Gizzy, how're you doing today?" She reached over and scratched the pig's head. She had no clue where Gizmo came from, but the best guess was that she was one of the many famous swimming pigs that inhabited Pig Beach in Exuma and had probably gotten caught in an undertow, cast out to sea, and miraculously ended up on her shore.

When she'd come across Gizmo lying on the sand, Kate and five of her staff had loaded her on Kate's fifty-foot luxury yacht and rushed her to a vet in Nassau. It was touch-and-go for a week, and had Kate not told them to do whatever it took to save her, and that money was not an issue, chances were that she never would have made it.

"You hungry for breakfast?" More low grunts and a few nods told her the answer to that question. She smiled as she scrubbed her fingers under Gizzy's chin, bent, and kissed her snout. "Come on, sweetie, I'll make a bowl of your favorites, then I think I'll go snorkel for a while."

Gizmo's grunting accelerated as Kate rolled out of the lounge chair, filled a bowl of vegetables, and grabbed her snorkel gear. She didn't bother to change out of her board shorts and sports bra. It was her standard attire these days. If she needed to do something at the resort, she threw on a Rainbow's End T-shirt and called it good enough. The days of spending over a thousand dollars on a pair of fashionably torn and distressed designer jeans that she would wear once before adding them to a pile of similar pants in one of her three walk-in closets, were gone. Now, the only things she really splurged on were water toys, her yacht being at the top of that list.

She walked on pristine white sand to the water's edge, put on her snorkel gear, and dove in. She was instantly greeted by an array of marine life that seemed unfazed by the sudden intrusion. She slowly kicked her fins and let the sun warm her back as she meandered over a patch of colorful coral. Her breathing slowed, and she let the solitude of being in the underwater world calm her mind.

As she rounded the northern tip of the cay, a large shark emerged from under a rocky ledge and rapidly closed the distance between them. Kate continued her slow methodical pace as the eight-foot shark glided next to her. She bit her mouthpiece as she smiled, extended her hand, and let her fingers glide gently over the rough skin. Bruce was the name Brooke had given to the resident nurse shark that had appeared one day and never left. No one feared Bruce, and he gave no reason to fear him. Clusters of nurse sharks were common in the area, but no one had ever seen one this close to the cay, much less making the area a permanent home. Bruce was obviously a bit of an outcast, and it was clear by the scars on his sides and the nicks in his fins that there was probably a reason for that.

After Brooke's death, he'd started to follow Kate around the reef. He'd trailed behind her, always maintaining his distance, until one day, he'd approached her side and joined her for a swim around the tip of the cay. She wasn't sure if he had picked up on some weird electrical pulse of grief coming from her or if he'd finally decided it was time to introduce himself. Either way, she had come to anticipate his company when she snorkeled the area and would be disappointed on the days he stayed under his ledge, resting and ignoring her.

Kate had never felt the need to try to make him some exotic pet. It wasn't about that for her. They were two souls silently swimming side by side, sharing a moment in time. Just a broken-hearted human and a shark that clearly looked as though he had seen better days.

When they made it to Kate's designated turnaround spot on the reef, Bruce continued on. She waved good-bye to him and returned to the shore, where Gizmo greeted her with a squeal and a circle of happiness.

"I love you too," she said as they headed to the house for companionship, snuggles, and another day that would end with a bowl of popcorn and a late-night movie.

Chapter Three

So you're really going to bury his urn at sea?" Allie's best friend, Reba, said as she sat across from her in a booth at the family's restaurant. "And before you answer that, can I just say you're killing it with this lentil loaf."

"Yeah, you like it?"

"Are you kidding? I think I could eat this all day, every day."

"Did you taste the ketchup? I made it from scratch."

Reba dipped a forkful of food into the sauce cup, devoured the bite, and moaned her reply.

"I know, right? I've been playing with some of the spices to give it a little more of a bold flavor."

Reba sat back and scrubbed her fingers on a paper napkin. "I know you've always hated working here and thought this place robbed you of your dream life, but now that you're in charge, think you'll finally restructure the menu?"

"I don't know. Dad was always so sure he would lose his customer base if he deviated from his signature dishes." Allie remembered the one and only time she'd mentioned that they should start incorporating healthier options. Her father had paused, turned to her, and with anger-laced words, told her that since his cooking hadn't killed him or her mother in all these years, it was obviously healthy enough. He'd ended their brief exchange with a warning to never criticize his menu choices again.

Reba snorted. "What signature dishes? Because I hate to break it to you, but baked mac and cheese, burgers and fries, tuna casserole, and chicken pot pie aren't exactly signature dishes."

Allie laughed, "Yeah." She leaned in. "But as you know, every dish comes with a heaping ladleful of the family's *secret sauce* on the side." She used air quotes for emphasis.

"Which consists of?"

"Flour, butter, cheddar cheese, heavy cream, and lots of salt. But shh." Allie pressed her finger against her lips. "It's our signature secret recipe." They both chuckled as she glanced around the comfort food diner. It was a small space that barely fit half a dozen booths and four average round tables. Red vinyl covered the seats, the tables were old-school linoleum, and a black-and-white checkered floor rounded out the seventies look that, according to an article she'd recently read online, was a style that was making a comeback.

"Is the place still struggling?"

Allie sighed and nodded. Even though their prices were cheap, the food was mediocre at best. The diner wasn't known for serving anything delicious, fancy, or unique. Just big plates full of the standard American classics. The portions filled people up, and although that kept a steady, but declining, flow of customers coming in the door, it never was enough to translate into anything more than dismal profits.

"Well, my vote is, ditch the cheese sauce and comfort foods, and focus on dishes like this one." Reba stabbed the lentil loaf. "And your business would probably double."

"That's what I'm hoping. When I get back from my trip, I'll have another talk with Mom about it. For now, she seems as reluctant to change the menu as Dad was."

"That's too bad because this is really tasty," Reba mumbled through another forkful of food. "Now, what time do you need me to pick you up in the morning?"

"My flight's at ten, so how about being at my place around six?"

"You excited?"

"About spending money that Mom needs so I can bury Dad on the ocean floor because of some dumb dream? No. About finally going on my first real vacation? Oh hell, yes. Plus, I haven't been diving since Shelly, so it'll be nice to get back in the water." Her ex was the co-owner of a dive shop in Long Beach, and the perk of that relationship was being taught all the ins and outs of scuba diving and operating a boat. Too bad their two-year relationship wasn't as enjoyable above the water as it was below.

"I still can't believe you contacted her. Especially after what she did to you."

"Yeah, I know. But one thing about Shelly, she seems to know everyone in the diving community. I figured she could steer me in the right direction when it came to renting a boat and gear in the Bahamas, and she did." When she'd told Shelly about her dad's death and her plans to bury his urn, she'd asked if Shelly knew anyone in that vicinity operating a dive shop. Shelly had said that yes, she did know someone and had reassured Allie she would take care of all the details and not to worry.

"Wouldn't it be wild if there really are signs that a battle took place there?"

"Seriously, Reba? I can't believe you actually said that."

"What? You never know what you might find."

"You know what I'm going to find? Sand. Lots of sand submerged in a lot of water, with no signs of anything else because there was never a battle, a tribe, or sunken canoes. This whole thing is ridiculous, and truthfully, I can't wait to finally put this part of my life to rest."

"Well, extra bonus points to your dad. Of all coordinates to tattoo on his chest, at least these take you to the Bahamas and not some frozen tundra or weird isolated shithole in the middle of nowhere."

"Yeah, that's true, and from the pics online, the water looks amazing. It'll be nice spending a week diving." Her mom had insisted she book enough time in the Bahamas to relax and unwind. That she deserved a break. Allie had initially baulked at the suggestion but quickly embraced the idea. It had been years since she'd been diving, and she missed the therapeutic sessions the underwater world provided. No matter how stressed or depressed she was, after just one dive, all her troubles seemed to melt away. She had never experienced anything that could transform her mood so quickly and completely. It was as though she found a part of her soul in the ocean, and more than once, she wished she could stay down there forever and never deal with her land life again.

"Don't go spending all your time diving. Remember to have fun hanging out with the ladies and enjoying the scene. I bet there's going to be some beautiful single women at the resort." Reba arched a brow.

"Reba."

"What? Oh, come on. A week in the Bahamas surrounded by a group of women? Please tell me that isn't the perfect place to hook up with someone."

"I'm not looking for a hookup. I'll be there on business."

"It'll take you what, an hour, tops, to bury the urn? That leaves six days and twenty-three hours left for the fun stuff. You deserve this vacation, and you deserve to get laid. I'm surprised your parts aren't rusting."

"Wow, you're in rare form today." But part of what Reba said was true. Allie had been feeling the itch to get back into the dating scene for a while. Her ego was no longer bruised from when Shelly had announced that she was breaking up with her because she was in love with an actress whose acting specialty primarily consisted of playing dead bodies in movies and TV shows and who, according to Shelly, had more depth and character than Allie did. She just wished Shelly had had the integrity to tell her about the affair before she had unexpectedly walked in on them one afternoon. In the fight that had ensued, Shelly was unapologetic and verbally abusive while her new lover played dead, and Allie reluctantly had to admit that the woman was pretty damn convincing.

"Allie," her mom called out with a wave.

Allie nodded an acknowledgement and turned back to Reba. "I gotta go. I still have a lot of prep to do before I leave."

"Go, go. I'll see you in the morning." She flicked her wrist and activated her smart watch. "Besides, I need to get going too. We're shooting in Santa Monica tonight in some neighborhood by the pier."

"Oh yeah? How's the movie going?"

"We're over budget, the director's an asshole, and one of the grips forgot to put his phone on vibrate during the big love scene, and it took hours before we could reshoot it because the lead actor said he lost his inspiration after the interruption. Let me tell you how well that went over." She shoveled another bite of food in her mouth. "God, I'm so tired of working low-budget films."

"Hey, your break will come. You're an amazing makeup artist."

Reba's cheeks flushed a bit as Allie scooted out of the booth. "You know I love it when you flirt with me. Now go." Reba shooed. "I'll see you in the morning."

"Thanks, Reba," Allie called over her shoulder as she hurried to her mom. "Yeah, Mom, what do you need?" But she knew the answer to that question before she even asked it.

"Go box up Charlie's leftovers," she said as she flicked her eyes toward a gaunt, elderly man sitting alone at his usual table. He was her dad's Army buddy, and he was a daily fixture at the diner. In fact, she had many fond childhood memories of sitting with Carlie at that very table while he read books to her as her parents tended to other customers.

"Hey, Charlie." She approached and gave his shoulder a loving squeeze. "Why don't I go box that up for you?" She reached for his plate as he nodded.

As she headed to the kitchen, she heard the familiar, "Thank you, dear" follow her through the swinging doors. This was the dance with Charlie. Every day he would come to the restaurant and order the special. He never finished, and when her mom would ask Allie to box up his leftovers, she knew that meant not only what was on his plate but enough to hold him over for the rest of the day. He had fallen on hard times, and his fixed social security income was not keeping up with the steady inflation and medical bills. Today, she scooped heaping portions of casserole in his container, added extra to-go cups of cheese sauce, and bagged everything up.

"Here you go, Charlie." She placed the bag on his table and helped him out of his chair.

"How much do I owe you?" He reached toward his back pocket.

"How about we put it on your tab, okay?" This too was part of their dance. When it came time to pay, he would always ask what he owed, and Allie would reassure him that they had a running bill that he could deal with later. A tab that was never created and would never come due.

He whispered more gratitude as Allie held the door for him. "We'll see you tomorrow, Charlie. Take care, okay?" She leaned against the door frame and protectively watched him lumber down the sidewalk. He was the last survivor of her dad's unit, and from the looks of him lately, it wouldn't be much longer before he and her dad would once again be reunited.

"I'll be in the office for a little while if anyone needs me," Allie announced as she headed toward the kitchen. The skeleton crew of two high school part-time helpers nodded as they fluttered around the restaurant, tending to the small handful of customers. They were in between the lunch and dinner crowd, and since the menu was the same for both, the food had been prepped since early that morning.

As she glided through the kitchen, she grabbed a glass and filled it with freshly brewed tea, then ducked into the closet-sized office next to the freezer. She maneuvered around bankers' boxes stacked and overflowing with paperwork, rocked back in the duct-taped, faded leather chair, and woke the computer on the gray metal desk.

When the screen came to life, she was greeted with a picture of a group of women dressed in bikinis on paddleboards, laughing at the camera and wearing Rainbow's End T-shirts and baseball hats. When she'd begun researching her father's coordinates, she'd realized she had a choice of two places to stay. Nassau was to the east and offered an impressive list of accommodations, sightseeing activities, multiple dive spots, including a cave, and of course, the famous Paradise Island, loaded with every amenity imaginable. She could devote a day to burying her dad and then take advantage of the tourist attractions the remainder of her time. To the west was a small, all-women resort on a private cay that lacked the array of attractions but offered her the opportunity to be amongst her own. Plus, it was a stone's throw from her father's coordinates, not that it mattered, but it was definitely an additional selling point.

The articles and reviews she'd pulled up raved about the Rainbow's End, and she was shocked when she'd learned the pricing for a week's stay was comparable, if not cheaper, than most of the hotels on Nassau. The pictures of the casitas were cute and charming, and the lagoon they faced was stunningly beautiful.

The resort booked reservations for every other week, a Saturday to a Saturday, and the place offered a complimentary yacht ride from Nassau that included resort swag, food, and free drinks to entertain the guests during the two-hour boat ride to the private cay. It was required that all guests who booked for that week needed to be on board the yacht at a precise time for departure, or the guest had to make other accommodations to get to the resort on their own.

When Allie had made her reservation, she'd checked the online box in the terms and agreement section that said she understood this when she declined the complimentary ride, since she would have her own boat, courtesy of Shelly's contact in Nassau. The email confirmation from the resort said she could moor her boat at their lagoon dock during the duration of her stay, and if she needed any additional accommodations, to let them know at least forty-eight hours in advance.

She sipped her tea as she moved her mouse over a second open tab. She had learned from researching the resort that it was owned by Kate Williams, rumored to be none other than the now elusive Suzanne Bennett. She clicked the folder, and pictures of Suzanne peppered the screen. She was stunning, even in the most unflattering paparazzi pictures. With her short, curly, sun-streaked blond hair and golden tan, she definitely embodied the stereotypic Southern California beauty. In most of the photos, she was dressed on the fashionably androgenous side and seemed to have a different woman on her arm in every picture. Allie knew the type. Those fortunate enough to have the spotlight shone on them basked in the attention, partied hard, and were full of themselves. And who they had dangling from their arm was nothing more than another accessory.

A quick search told her that she and Suzanne had an age gap of almost eight years, and although they'd grown up in relative proximity, the difference in their zip codes meant that they were worlds apart. She took another sip and clicked on several pictures when she noticed that about ten years ago, the photos of *Bad Girl Bennett* stopped. In the last one posted, Suzanne had her hand up to the camera, head tilted down, and clearly looked tired of being harassed by the paparazzi. Allie wondered what it would be like to be one of the few who were deemed worthy enough to be hounded by those who made a buck by shoving a camera in someone's personal space and selling their image. Where one's privacy was traded for scandalous headlines that consumers seemed to not only love but devour. *No thanks. I'll take my life over that any day, although the money would sure be nice.*

She clicked on her last open tab. The one labeled "Kate Williams." A British gossip magazine she had never heard of had run a small story about the Bennett family transferring the deed to their private island in the Bahamas to their one and only daughter. It was also rumored, according to the tabloid, that Suzanne Bennett had legally changed her name to Kate Williams. She clicked the dozen or so images the magazine posted and stared at the semi-blurry photos, obviously taken from an offshore boat, of a woman walking on a beach and lounging on the patio of a large estate home. In two of the photos, she was accompanied by another woman. It was hard to tell if the person in the photos was really Suzanne Bennett, but even so, what would cause her to want to separate from the family name? She had won the birth lottery by being born wealthy and privileged. Why run from that?

❖

The flight to Miami was smooth and uneventful, and Allie was grateful to be able to sleep most of the duration. She was exhausted from staying up most of the night prepping the restaurant as much as possible for her week away. It wasn't as though she had never taken time away from the diner before, but short trips with girlfriends up to San Francisco for a weekend of fun running around Pier 39 or down to San Diego for a day were nothing like this. This was the first time she was going to be so far away, on her own, and for such a lengthy period.

She grabbed her phone as she headed to a departure screen, scanned it until she found her connecting flight to Nassau, and headed for the designated gate as she hit her mom's number.

"Is that the right button...I don't have my glasses on, did I..."

"Ma?"

"Hello?"

"Hey, Mom, the plane was delayed taking off from LAX, so I'm running to my connecting flight, but I just wanted to let you know I'm in Miami."

"How wonderful. I was just telling Charlie here about your trip. Say hi, Charlie, it's Allie."

"Hi," Charlie's soft voice was barely audible.

"Charlie says hi," her mom said.

"Yes, I heard. Tell Charlie hi back," she said as she picked up her pace and huffed. She had ten minutes to get to gate twenty-three, and she was only at gate twelve. "How are things going?"

"Fine, just fine. How's your father?"

"He made it through all the security checks." Allie had double-checked to make sure the urn they had her dad's ashes in was travel safe and that all the proper documents were in hand. "Um, hey, Ma, I gotta go," she said as pre-boarding for her flight was announced. "I'll check in again when I arrive in Nassau, okay?" She began jogging down the concourse. "Oh, and Sam told me to tell you he'd swing by the restaurant around nine to pick you up." Fortunately, her cousin had agreed to stay with her mom while she was on vacation, so thankfully, that was one less thing she had to worry about.

"That's fine, dear, go catch your flight. We'll talk later."

"Okay bye, Mom. I'll call you—"

"Oh, for heaven's sake, did I just press the wrong button… Charlie, take a look…" And with those words, the line went dead.

Allie chuckled as she dodged people while sprinting the remaining few yards to her gate and the small twelve passenger plane that would shuttle her to Nassau.

"Just in time," the cheery voice of the flight attendant said as she scanned the QR code on Allie's phone.

As she strolled down the aisle of the shuttle plane, she glanced at her ticket and paired it with seat 6A. She settled in, pushed herself deep into the cushion, buckled up, and took a moment to glance around the cabin. Flying had always unnerved her, so back-to-back flights was causing her anxiety to ramp up a bit. She let out a shaky breath and reminded herself that according to the statistics, she was more likely to die from being attacked by a cow than in a plane crash.

She stowed her backpack under the seat and when the plane pushed away from the gate, she gave it a loving tap. "Almost there, Dad," she said to herself as she tried to steady her nerves. "Almost there," she repeated as the plane accelerated down the runway, lifted into clear skies, and quickly banked left.

After a short, uneventful flight, a slight delay in customs, and a shuttle service that was thirty minutes late picking her up because apparently, island time was a real thing in the Bahamas, she was standing on a run-down dock in Coral Harbour.

"You're kidding. There must be a mistake because that can't be the boat I rented." She glanced at Olivia, the California transplant that Shelly set her up with, as dread filled her stomach. "That thing looks twice as old as I am." The boat was the color combination of rust stains over weathered blue paint and was so small, two people would have to waltz around each other to go from stern to bow.

"I know she doesn't look like much, but don't let looks fool you. She's my baby, and she's plenty seaworthy." Olivia beamed. "She'll get you where you need to be and back with no worries."

And yet, as Allie stood speechless, staring at the tiny fishing boat that looked like it would barely make a lap around a child's water park ride, she seriously doubted it. "Um." She turned to Olivia. "I'm sorry, I don't mean to be rude or anything, but did you just say this is *your* boat?"

"Yep, bought her from a retired fisherman who was going to scrap her. I rebuilt her myself." The words were full of pride. "But I haven't gotten around to painting her yet."

Allie let out a breath to try to curb the anger and anxiety building inside her. "Back up. Shelly said you owned a dive shop, and you had a fleet of thirty footers. One of which, I was under the assumption that I was renting. Why didn't you tell me in the email exchange that this is what I was getting instead? Or you know, send a picture, a brief description, the original obituary notice of the boat before you decided to resurrect her…anything that would give me a heads-up that this is what I was in for instead of one of the thirty footers your shop pictures on its website." She didn't mean to be snarky or hurt Olivia's feelings, but she was tired and bordering on bitchy. Strike that. Based on the look Olivia was now giving her, she must have officially crossed over to the bitchy zone.

Olivia took off her baseball cap, letting her long black hair fall around her shoulders as she scratched at her scalp and averted her eyes. "I'm so sorry about that. The dive shop does have a fleet of thirty footers, but I, um, I'm kinda…" She stuttered, took a long breath, and gazed at her with apologetic eyes. "I just work there as a dive instructor. When I told Shelly I could rent you a boat, I may have left out a few details."

"Ya think?" Allie snapped.

"But for the price Shelly said you wanted to pay, there's no way you'd be able to rent that kind of boat plus the dive equipment for a week." She threw the statement out as an obvious attempt to justify her actions.

"I'm sorry, can we just…can we back up again and review the part where you said you *work* at the dive shop. As in, you're not part *owner* of the dive shop?"

Again, Olivia averted her eyes. "I may have overstated my position to Shelly."

"Obviously," Allie bit back as she folded her arms tightly across her chest and glared. "I need to know what's going on here. The truth, Olivia." When Shelly had said she could set Allie up with someone she knew in Nassau and had reassured her that she would take care of the details, Allie should have known better.

Olivia paused as she kicked at a knot that was sticking out of a plank on the weathered wood pier. "Did Shelly mention to you that we're exes?"

"No. Seems like a lot of details were left out regarding this whole setup. And I'm not quite sure what that has to do with me renting a boat and dive gear." Allie aggressively swatted at a bug that was on a suicide mission if it continued violating her airspace as her irritation began to boil over. Why was it that everything that happened in Shelly's orbit turned out to be so fucked-up?

"Yeah, well, Shelly and I were together for over two years. She broke up with me to be with someone whose family owned several Mercedes dealerships in San Diego, and I interpreted that as Shelly wanting to be with someone who had more money than I did." She took a breath, then locked eyes with Allie. "It made me feel inferior, as though I wasn't good enough for her standards. So when we ran into each other at a scuba convention last year, and she asked me how I was doing, I told her I co-owned a dive shop in Nassau. I don't know why I lied, the words just kinda flew out of my mouth. I know that was petty and childish, but it was worth it to see the shock on her face and hear the stumble in her voice. I could tell her wheels were spinning over that one." She snorted, then scrunched her brow in a sorrowful expression. "Sorry that me wanting to stick it to Shelly got in the way of being up-front with you. I just didn't know how close you two are, and I didn't want it getting back to her. In fact, I was going to ask you to please keep this on the down-low and between us."

This whole thing was bullshit, but Allie couldn't help giving an understanding nod. "We're not close, so you don't have to worry about that. In fact, she broke up with me to be with an actress who makes her living playing dead bodies in crime shows. Deep down, I think Shelly's desire to be with someone who has a connection to the major studios was more attractive than the woman she dumped me for. Either way, it was something a cook for her family's small restaurant in east LA couldn't offer her."

Olivia threw her head back in laughter and placed a gentle hand on Allie's shoulders. "Looks like we've both been *Shelly'd*. I'm sorry she did that to you, and I'm sorry I let some of my lingering anger toward her get the better of my character. But I would never rent you a boat or gear that I wasn't completely confident in. Now come on, let me show you around *Betty*."

"*Betty*? Seriously?" she said as she hopped aboard behind Olivia.

"It's a long story that involved way too much tequila. But I'm telling you, what she lacks in beauty, she makes up for in heart. She's got a brand-new motor, and last month, I rewired all the electronics, put in a Wi-Fi booster, and added a new Bluetooth Chartplotter computer that'll get you anywhere you need to go day or night. Trust me, she'll take care of you...I promise."

Olivia gave Allie the ins and outs of the vessel, which took all of about ten minutes. "And here are your tanks." She pointed to four silver cylinders strapped in the stern of the boat. "Aluminum, eighty-cubic-footers, just like you requested," she said as she tapped them. "And your scuba package is in here." She lifted the lip of a green and white storage bin that looked like a big cooler and was bolted down next to the tanks. "It's all top-of-the-line equipment, and like I told Shelly, I gave you the friends and family employee discount on everything. So I hope that makes up a little for misleading you about the boat."

Olivia hopped off, allowing Allie the opportunity to glance over the equipment. She trailed her fingers over the cylinders and shivered as the cool touch of aluminum reminded her of the love she held in her heart for the hobby. She made a promise to herself that when she returned home, she would somehow find the time and money to join a scuba club, then made a second promise to keep the first.

She pulled a few items out of the bin and nodded her approval. "This is actually really nice. I'm impressed." She felt her anger subside as the thrill of being back in the water emerged. "Wait, what's this?" She tugged at a handle to free the device from the bottom of the pile.

"It's a metal detector."

"I didn't order a metal detector."

"It's our special of the month. Our boss thought it would be a good marketing gimmick for anyone renting our gear package for five days or more. A lot of divers come here to search for lost treasures. Especially since the recent hurricanes have really churned up the water. In fact, quite a lot of social media influencers have been posting videos of themselves diving all around here to see if the storms uncovered any hidden secrets."

"Oh yeah, anyone find anything?" Allie had read about the age of piracy in the Bahamas and how Nassau was once known as the Republic of Pirates. With colorful stories of how Blackbeard and Calico Jack would hide in the shallow waters, hidden behind island foliage, and ambush merchant ships. And legend had it that millions upon millions of buried, sunken, and hidden treasures were scattered throughout the islands and waterways, just waiting to be unearthed by modern-day treasure hunters.

Olivia shrugged. "Not really, but tourists seem to love trying. There'll always be someone hoping to be lucky enough to be *the one*." A comfortable silence fell between them as she handed Allie her luggage. "You're taking her over to the Rainbow's End, huh?"

"Yep." Allie placed her suitcase next to the gear box and shrugged out of her backpack.

"I've always wanted to work at that resort." Olivia said as she untied the mooring line and tossed it to Allie.

"Oh yeah, why don't you?"

"Never an opening. Guess everyone likes it there."

"Well, if I hear of something, I'll put in a good word for you." Allie waved good-bye, typed in the coordinates of the resort in the Chartplotter, throttled forward, and headed southwest. It was a beautiful sunny day, the temperature was mild, and the air smelled of salt instead of car exhaust. Her blood pressure felt like it dropped several digits, and as she stood at the controls of the boat, letting the sea air blow over her, she thought about Suzanne Bennett. If she really had changed her name and run away to a private cay, Allie couldn't blame her. Compared to Los Angeles—hell, compared to anywhere she'd been—this place seemed like paradise.

CHAPTER FOUR

K ate stood beside Carla on the deck of her yacht, now docked in the vicinity of the Nassau Cruise Port. She took a moment to glance at a few of the cruise ships moored, full of passengers experiencing all the amenities a floating city had to offer. She smiled at a distant memory of herself as a child having those same enchanting expectations every time she'd joined her parents, and the company's senior leaders and major stockholders' families, on their annual Bahama cruise. In a deal with a major cruise line, Bennett Enterprises would charter one of their ships for a week and enjoy a leisurely private voyage around the islands, complete with all the bells, whistles, and packaged excursions. It was the one time a year when they'd come together as a family unit, if only for the sake of appearance, and Kate could pretend that all was well in her little messed-up and dysfunctional world.

During their fourth visit to the Bahamas, her parents had heard about a private cay with a beautiful house set into a hillside that was on the market for, according to their Realtor friend, "a steal." They'd made a cash offer based on the photos, and four weeks later, they were the proud owners of their very own tropical island. They talked of taking vacations there, and for a brief moment, Kate had actually believed in the fantasy and illusion of them all coming together as one happy family. But reality had a harsh way of storming in and slashing at her dreams until there was nothing left but shattered pieces of unrecognizable hope scattered at her feet. There was never a family trip to the island. In fact, the only time the Bahamas house had been occupied was when she'd wanted a break from the LA scene and had brought whoever was dangling on her arm at that moment over for a week of sex and partying. And more times than not, she would slip out of the house late at night when her temporary girlfriend was sleeping and settle into a patio lounge chair, stare into the darkness of the ocean, and wish her family life resembled a Norman Rockwell painting instead of a Pollock. But no matter how much she wanted love and stability in her life, it apparently just wasn't meant to be.

"Here comes Anthony." Carla's words brought her back to the present as she focused on the white passenger van headed in their direction with *Anthony's Shuttle Service* painted on the side.

When Carla had approached Kate and Brooke several years ago and had asked if there was any way the resort could recommend her struggling cousin's one-person Nassau taxi company for rides to and from the dock, Brooke and Kate had done one better. They'd put him on a retainer, bought him a new passenger van, and incorporated his service into their complimentary amenities package. Since most guests needed a ride to the dock from the Lynden Pindling International Airport or several of the surrounding hotels, they had Anthony gather them up from their various locations and shuttle them to the yacht and reversed the trip one week later when they returned.

Kate turned to Carla. "Is everyone accounted for?"

"Yep. Anthony texted and said everyone's aboard."

The van came to a stop, and seven women spilled out. They were chatty and smiling, and Kate thought they looked like a fun group.

"Welcome aboard." She waved them over and helped each one onto the yacht as Carla checked off their names, and Anthony loaded their luggage. When everyone was settled, Carla turned to her cousin and greeted him with a warm hug. "Hey, cuz."

"Anthony." Kate approached with her customary handshake stuffed with a hundred-dollar tip. "How's Julie doing?" she asked of his wife and her third pregnancy.

"She's well, and the doctor said we're still on schedule for a March twenty-eighth delivery."

"Another Aries brought into this world." Carla shook her head. "God help us all."

"What are you talking about? You're an Aries." Kate chuckled.

"Exactly," Carla said. "So I already know that kid's going to be a handful."

"Well, if she turns out anything like you, she'll be a joy," Kate reassured and silently thanked the stars yet again for bringing Carla into her life ten years ago.

Brooke had heard about Carla after an LGBTQ+ advocate group on Nassau had reached out about a bright, young, twenty-two-year-old, trans woman disowned by her family, mistreated, misunderstood, and homeless. Down on her luck, she had resorted to stealing food for survival, but her debut attempt into criminal life had ended after the minimart owner had tackled her and roughed her up pretty bad when he'd caught her trying to make a quick escape with a hotdog, a bag of chips, and a soda. The group had known that if she went to prison, she wouldn't last long in the system. She needed a break, not jail time.

When Kate and Brooke had been introduced to Carla, she was sitting hunched against the back cement wall in a ten-by-ten holding cell with tearstained streaks cutting through a bloody, bruised, and dirty face. Her clothes were tattered and torn, and she smelled like she hadn't showered in weeks.

"She just needs a second chance and an opportunity to crawl out of her hole," the advocate had told them. "I talked the judge into letting her off with a warning, but he won't release her until someone posts bail."

At first, Kate wasn't in agreement when Brooke had suggested they not only pay her bail but create a position for her at the resort. When Kate had hesitated, Brooke had reminded her that the only reason *she* hadn't ended up in jail was because of her family's high-priced lawyers, something Carla was not fortunate enough to have. Reluctantly, Kate had agreed, and Carla became the newest crew member to join the Rainbow's End.

She soon proved herself as a hard worker who was passionate and proud of her new job as the resort's handywoman, or as Brooke so fondly called it, the resort's honey-do woman. Anyone who needed help or assistance called on Carla. She was intelligent, articulate, had a wicked sense of humor, and within a few months, knew the ins and outs of every aspect of the resort and had already made several suggestions on how to improve their business model.

Two years later, for her twenty-fourth birthday, she'd flown to Miami to undergo the surgery she'd so desperately wanted. Kate and Brooke had covered all expenses, and even though Carla had insisted they take money out of her salary until the bills were paid back in full, they'd never docked a single penny from her pay.

After Brooke died, Kate had asked Carla to take over managing the resort. She'd taught her how to operate the yacht so she could drop off and pick up the guests in Nassau while Kate closed herself off from the world. Carla had risen to the occasion and shined in her new role. The guests loved her, the staff respected her, and Kate trusted her. And on the days when the rabbit hole that had become Kate's life felt impossible to crawl out of, Carla watched over her like a mama bear. She brought her food several times a day, was relentless at checking in, and even slept on her patio the evenings when Kate seemed less responsive.

Yes, she acknowledged as she glanced at Carla interacting with the guests. She was so much more than just the manager of the resort; she was a true friend. A best friend, and that was something Kate had never had in her life.

"Ladies, my name is Kate Williams. I am the owner of Rainbow's End, but Carla here is the one who runs the place, so anything you need during your stay, please let her know, and we will address it immediately. In the meantime, please make yourselves comfortable while we head to the cay. Drinks, snacks, and a welcome bag with T-shirts and baseball caps are over there." Kate waved in the direction of a banquet table. "If anyone is a little sensitive to the boat's motion, we have patches, just hit us up for those. Bathrooms are down below…and what else? Oh yeah, please let us know if you see any dolphins, whales, turtles, or other aquatic life so we can slow the boat and take a few minutes to enjoy watching them. I think that covers it…welcome aboard."

The chatter and cheers went up a notch as Carla escorted them to the food and started handing out gift bags of swag. Kate headed to the helm, settled into the black leather seat, touched an icon on one of several computer screens, and the beat of the first song on her playlist surrounded the boat.

She glanced over her shoulder as she powered up the yacht, and between the mingling and laughter, everyone looked like they were already having fun. Kate viewed this time on the boat as an important one for the guests because for the next couple of hours, it gave them a chance to get to know one another. And more times than not, by the end of the week, most had made lifelong friendships.

She bobbed her head and began mouthing the lyrics to one of her favorite eighties' tunes as she eased the boat out of the harbor and headed for the only place she had ever felt at home.

❖

The trip back to the resort took longer than usual after stopping twice: once to enjoy the antics of a pod of bottlenose dolphins and again after one of the guests spotted a family of humpback whales with a calf. Kate called Jo, the resort's assistant manager, to let her know they were running a little late and to pass the word on to Chef Mila so she could delay the serving of dinner another hour. Yes, she knew that was going to piss Mila off, and yes, she also knew she would get an earful later tonight. But the guests appreciated the opportunity to see something most of them had never seen in their lifetimes.

By the time they approached the cay, the staff had gathered, waiting to moor the boat, greet the new guests, help with their luggage, and transport them in golf carts to their casitas. Carla and Kate held back to perform their routine walk-through of the yacht and make sure nothing was left behind. When all looked good, they disembarked.

"Looks like the last of the guests has arrived." Carla tilted her chin in the direction of Allie's boat.

"Yeah, I noticed." Kate purposely kept her tone flat as she headed over to the boat and shook her head. "Man, this thing has seen better days. How the hell did she make it here from Nassau in this?" She craned her neck and glanced around the boat, then hopped aboard.

Carla waved a scolding finger. "And what the hell do you think you're doing? That ain't your boat to be snooping around on."

"Nope, but it's tied to my dock. Besides, I'm not snooping, I'm just politely glancing around," Kate mumbled as she turned in a three-sixty, still amazed that the vessel was seaworthy. She approached the stern and let her fingers gently glide over the four scuba cylinders as she cocked her head in curiosity toward the storage bin. For a brief moment, she thought it would be rude and unprofessional to peek inside but just as quickly dismissed her thoughts as she bent and raised the lid. "Shit," she groaned as her stomach bottomed out. "She's a treasure hunter." Kate's anger and anxiety burned through her as she stood staring at the metal detector.

"And how do you know that?" Carla shot back in an accusatory tone as she folded her arms.

Kate reached in, pulled out the device and held it up for display.

Carla's expression softened. "So, not a recreational diver, after all." She raised a brow.

Kate shook her head as she returned the metal detector, leaned against the side of the boat, and scrubbed her fingers through her hair. "Shit," she repeated as her mind raced with the possibilities of this reality.

"What do you want me to do, boss?"

"Nothing." She hopped off the boat. "I'm going to go officially welcome her to the resort and let her know I won't tolerate treasure hunting in these waters." If there were sunken fortunes out there, Kate wanted nothing to do with the attention they would bring. She had a nice life on the island. It was calm, drama free, and she enjoyed the guests and loved her staff. Things were working well, and she didn't want anything or anyone upsetting that rhythm.

Only once in all the years of running the resort had she kicked someone off the island. That was two years ago after a woman had seen Gizmo and made several offhanded snarky comments like, the only good thing about a pig was when they ended up as bacon on a burger, and had followed it up with wanting to know if Gizmo was the main attraction in a luau. Kate was so furious, she'd hired a plane to get the guest off the island and back to Nassau as fast as she could. As Kate headed to Casita Four, she hoped it wouldn't come to that.

CHAPTER FIVE

A llie lay on the bed in her casita with her eyes closed. It had been a long couple of days. Hell, who was she kidding, it had been a long several months. Between the time her dad was diagnosed with terminal cancer until now, she'd felt like she had been on a nauseating and exhausting never-ending roller coaster ride. And now that she was finally on the cay, instead of feeling energized, she was feeling the weight of it all pressing on her. *Sometimes, you don't realize how tired you are until you stop running.*

She heard the chatter of the other guests arriving and settling into the casitas around her, but instead of going out and introducing herself, she opted to unpack and take a nap before dinner. Tomorrow, she would lay her father to rest, and maybe after that, she would be more in the mood to mingle.

The ringing of her phone sent her scrambling to remember where she'd left it. She followed the ringtone to her backpack that was perched on the couch, fumbled for it, and barely beat the voice mail.

"Hey, Reba." She yawned as she stumbled back to the bed.

"Someone sounds sleepy," Reba said.

"I think I dozed off." Allie rubbed at her eyes and tried to bring the room and her thoughts into focus.

"You dozed off? You just texted me…what…less than an hour ago that you arrived and were safe and sound after your boat rental fiasco on Nassau. Why aren't you on the beach having tropical drinks with the other women?"

"Because I'm exhausted, and I wanted to take a nap."

"I'm sorry, I couldn't hear you while I was playing my sympathy violin. So let me repeat myself in case I wasn't clear the first time. You are in the Bahamas surrounded by women, you have only one week, and you're still in your casita? I'm seriously starting to question our friendship."

"All right, all right." She groaned in a lighthearted way. "I'll shake it off and join in the festivities. Happy now?"

"That's my girl. Now, catch me up."

Allie yawed again as she scooted toward the top of the bed, propped up some pillows, and leaned her back against the headboard. "Well, the cay is gorgeous. Before I docked, I circled it to get a feel of the place. I saw a private house on the far north side, our casitas are on the far south side, and the resort is kinda in the middle, facing the most beautiful cove I've ever seen. The surrounding water is clear and shallow, and I can already tell there's plenty of sea life."

"Sweetie, I don't care about the sea life. What I care about is the resort life. Did you meet any of the other women yet? Any of them seem interesting?"

"Reba, I just got here. But I must admit, the cutest butch I've ever seen tied me up when I arrived."

Allie yanked the phone from her ear as Reba squealed. "Oh my God, Allie, you already had sex? Why didn't you lead with that?"

"What?"

"You said a butch tied you up."

"The boat, Reba, she tied up the boat."

"Oh, for fuck's sake, who cares about the boat? Don't go teasing me like that."

"I didn't tease you. Your mind just naturally drifted to—" A soft knock on the door interrupted her. "Hold on, Reba, someone's knocking."

The moment Allie opened the door, her breath caught. The hair was a bit shorter, the body thinner, and her tan darker, but there was no denying those crystal blue eyes that held her in a trance. The tabloid pictures definingly didn't do them justice.

"Allie?"

Allie nodded, at least she thought she did because her mind still felt momentarily frozen. God, the woman was gorgeous in all the ways that made her body stand at attention.

"I'm Kate Williams." Kate's hand was extended in her direction as another squeal was emitted from her phone. The moment Allie wrapped her fingers around Kate's, her stomach tingled from the jolt of attraction. "I, um…hi, it's a pleasure to meet you."

She heard Reba's muffled, "What's happening? What's going on?" Allie held up a finger to signal she needed a moment while she pressed her phone to her ear. "Reba, I need to call you back."

"Is that her? Is that Suzanne Bennett? What's she like… you have to tell me everything that…" Reba rapid fired the questions as Allie disconnected the call.

"I'm sorry to bother you, but since you arrived before we got back from Nassau with the other guests, I haven't had the opportunity to introduce myself. I'm the owner of Rainbow's End and I thought I'd go over the ins and outs of the resort with you."

Allie motioned for Kate to enter. "I called the number listed on my confirmation email to let someone know I was arriving, and Jo met me at the dock, settled me in, and gave me the rundown on everything." She took a seat on the couch and motioned for Kate to do the same, but she waved her off.

"Ah, yes...Jo. If you need paddleboard lessons or want to snorkel around the lagoon during your stay, she's your guide. But I know you're a diver, so shall I assume that snorkeling is not your thing?"

"I actually love snorkeling, but yes, of the two, I do prefer diving. Do you dive?"

"I free dive."

"Wow, that's impressive. What depth and for how long?"

"Thirty to forty feet and upward of three minutes. But..." Kate waved a dismissive hand as she frowned and averted her eyes. "I haven't done it in a while."

"Why not?"

Kate stared at Allie, and the eyes that moments ago had seemed to sparkle now held an almost haunting glaze to them. "I just haven't. Anyway...I also wanted to stop by and make sure you're fully aware of our diving policy."

"Your diving policy?"

"Yes. For the most part, the water in the Bahamas is clear and the sea life abundant. Jo could probably fill you in on the best spots to dive, and as you probably know, there are several ship and plane wrecks that are not too far from here that have become popular with tourists. But if you had any intention of treasure hunting in close proximity to the cay, I must ask you to refrain. It's a resort policy that treasure hunting is strictly forbidden."

"Treasure hunting?" Allie lightheartedly laughed as she shook her head and remembered what Olivia had said about the influx of amateur hunters to hit the area since their last hurricane. "I can assure you that I won't be doing any treasure hunting. That's not why I'm here."

Kate cocked her head. "Oh?"

Allie fidgeted a bit while she glanced at her backpack. There really wasn't any reason not to tell Kate about her dad's wish, yet there was equally no reason to tell her. It was a private matter, and besides, his coordinates put his burial spot far enough from the cay that it shouldn't make a difference to Kate one way or another.

"I'm here to enjoy the resort and take some time to scuba dive, something I haven't had an opportunity to do in years because work and life's obligations always seem to get in the way."

"Oh yeah, what do you do? If you don't mind my asking?"

"I help run my family's small restaurant in LA."

"Ah, then I will be more than curious to know what you think of Mila's cooking. She's our chef, and she's a master at spices and sauces."

"Wonderful, you've given me another reason to look forward to dinner," Allie said with the assumption that Kate would be joining in the dining festivities.

"Well, then…" Kate trailed off, and Allie couldn't help feeling a bit exposed in the awkward silence that fell between them as she sensed Kate checking her out. "I'll let you get back to whatever it was you were doing. They'll be serving dinner in ten minutes, and thank you for understanding about our policy of no treasure hunting."

"Yeah, totally, no worries. I promise you, I won't be doing any treasure hunting while I'm here."

"Thank you."

"You're welcome. See you at dinner?" she said with hope as she escorted Kate back to the door.

Kate turned. "No. I don't dine with the guests."

"Oh. That's, um, too bad," she said hoping her disappointment wasn't apparent in her tone. "Another resort policy?"

Kate shook her head. "My policy," she said in a soft tone. "Enjoy your evening, Allie." Kate turned to walk away but not before pausing and locking eyes one more time with her. A slight chill flushed Allie's body, causing goose bumps to form on her skin. They connected, she thought, in that wordless way people did when all their innermost senses were pinged.

"Thanks...you as well." Allie closed the door and leaned against the wall. Wow, what was that? She had been attracted to Kate in the pictures, but in person, she was stunning. Truly stunning. And was the connection she felt one of mutual attraction? She momentarily closed her eyes and hoped the answer was yes. That even though she had been out of the dating scene for several years, she could still read the room when it came to sexual energy.

Another knock on the door sent her lunging for the knob. She quickly opened it, expecting Kate.

"Hey."

"Hey...Jo." She let out the anticipation she'd held in her breath and relaxed. "What's up?"

Jo lingered in the doorway. "So, um, I was wondering if I could escort you to dinner. We'll be serving soon, and Mila, that's our chef, is an incredible cook. If you've never had fried plantains before, you're in for a treat."

Allie remembered seeing them on the menu the resort had emailed to her. It listed every meal that would be served at each seating. If she wanted to add something to the preplanned menu, she could submit a special request from their list of substitute dishes. Allie recalled plantains being a part of every evening meal. "I love plantains." In fact, she and Reba would frequent a restaurant in West Hollywood and only order side dishes of the fried fruit.

"Well, just wait until you've had Mila's. She has some type of spice she sprinkles on them that makes them the best you've probably ever had."

"That's quite the endorsement." Allie moaned as her hunger pangs began overpowering her fatigue. "Do I need to bring anything?"

"Your phone if you want to take pictures, but other than that, no."

Allie sent off a text to Reba, telling her she was headed to dinner, and she'd text more later. "Okay, I'm ready." She pocketed her phone.

The sun was low on the horizon, so the full effect of the tiki-torchlit path was not yet fully realized as they meandered past the other casitas. They engaged in small talk until they reached an area by the lagoon where a long banquet table was draped with white linen. A cluster of tealight flameless candles glowed, and the close proximity to the ocean made the ambiance breathtaking.

Five other guests were already seated, and as Allie approached, Jo pulled out a chair for her. "Hey everyone, this is Allie," she announced, then bent and whispered in her ear. "If you need anything, just holler. Enjoy your dinner."

Allie thanked her, and a momentary feeling of awkwardness washed over her as the women—who were as pale as the white T-shirts they were all wearing—focused on her.

"Hi, Allie," the one sitting closest to her piped up. "I'm Linda, this here's Jan, Sheri, Deb, and Barbara." She pointed as she introduced those around her. "If you can't remember our names, we also answer to 'Hey, Canadian.'" Linda tugged at her shirt, pulling at the large red maple leaf dead center. "Gotta represent, ya know?" She leaned close to Allie and snapped a selfie. "Where're you from?" she asked as she focused on her phone.

"Los Angeles."

"There, Allie from LA," Linda mumbled as she turned her screen around. "I just posted our pic so that means we're officially friends."

Allie's feelings of being an outsider were eased. She could tell this group, and especially Linda, was going to be fun to hang out with during her stay.

"So you weren't on the boat from Nassau. What's up with that?" Linda asked as a basket of rolls was placed on the table, causing Allie's mouth to water at the wonderful smell wafting her way. She wanted to reach out and grab one but refrained out of politeness.

"Linda," Jan said, "don't you think that's a bit personal?"

"What? We're friends now, so we can ask inappropriate personal questions. Right?" She leaned over and nudged Allie's shoulder.

"Don't feel like you have to answer her," Jan reassured. "She has a tendency to overstep her boundaries at times."

Allie waved dismissively. "No worries. Actually, I will be doing some diving while I'm here, so I rented a boat from Nassau and brought it over." She refrained from pointing out the obvious, that the embarrassingly dumpy-looking vessel docked opposite the gorgeous yacht was, in fact, her boat.

"No shit? You're a diver, huh?" Jan said.

Allie nodded. "I am, are you?"

"Are you kidding?" Linda snorted. "Jan is scared shitless of sharks, so being out in water deeper than a kiddie pool would make her crap her bikini bottoms."

"That's not true." Jan threw a roll. Linda ducked, and the puffed dough hit Jo in the chest and bounced to the ground.

"Settle down, kids," Jo said in a lighthearted way as she and several other members of the staff approached from behind and placed huge bowls of food in front of them. "Or I'm going to have to separate you." She winked at Allie. "Okay, ladies, as you know, we serve family style here, so take what you want and pass it around. The bowls are full of pasta, and that tray,"—she pointed—"has the plantains and the other one the sauteed asparagus and onions. Our chef likes to bulk cook, so any leftovers can be boxed up so you can take them back to your casitas to munch on later. Enjoy."

"What about the honeymooners? Shouldn't we wait for them?"

"They requested room service."

"Ooo," the table knowingly cooed as they nodded. "Well, then." Linda grabbed a bowl and dug in. "No sense letting this get cold." She plopped a heaping spoonful of pasta dripping in tomato sauce on her plate, then motioned to Allie if she wanted the same.

Allie nodded, and as Linda filled her plate, she reached for a roll. Bowls and trays were passed back and forth until Allie's plate was overflowing. If everything tasted half as good as it smelled, she knew she was in for a treat. She shoveled a forkful into her mouth, chased it with a bite of the roll, and her senses came alive. She had been playing with spice combinations a lot the past few weeks in an attempt to make her family's cheese sauce recipe more appealing. She'd spent hours on YouTube taking notes from cooking influencers as they shared their secrets on making flavorful sauces and mixing the right combination of spices, but nothing she had ever tried lit up her tastebuds like this. Each bite, each savory mouthful, was like introducing her to a sensation she had never known.

"Everything okay?" Jo said as she swung by the table. "Anyone need anything?"

"Jo, this food is amazing," Allie mumbled as she chewed. "Everything is so tasty. And you were right about the plantains. They're delicious."

"Told ya."

"Seriously, what kind of spices does the chef use?"

"Ah, for that answer, you'll have to ask Mila herself. But be warned, she's a feisty one. I'll let her know you like her cooking."

"I more than like it. I love it."

Jo paused for a moment and lingered. "Allie, I was kinda wondering. After you're done eating, I could show you around the cay a bit and give you some of the history of the Bahamas. If you'd like?" Her cheeks were beginning to flush, and Allie thought it was endearing that such a confident-looking woman seemed so shy about asking her to go for a walk.

"I think that would be wonderful." Allie gazed into Jo's hopeful expression. She would rather have Kate give her a history lesson, but Jo was adorable and someone she got a good vibe from. A friendship with her she was comfortable with, but anything more than that was something she wasn't interested in.

"Really?" Jo beamed as she backed away. "Awesome. I'll, um, I'll swing back by after you're done with dessert."

"Yeah, okay. That would be great." Allie returned to her meal, and she could see from the corner of her eye that all the Canadians were staring at her.

"What?" Allie said through a mouthful of plantains as she glanced around the table. "Do I have something on my face?" She wiped the napkin over her mouth.

"Yes, you have something on your face. It's called a smattering of lustful glee," Linda said. "And don't act coy with us. We're your friends now. We can openly gossip about the fact that that fine specimen of a woman is into you."

"Jo? Oh, I think she's just being hospitable." Allie lied because she wasn't that clueless. Her senses had already been pinging into the warning zone that Jo would probably be wanting more.

"I think her 'hospitality' extends to just you because she sure as shit didn't ask me if I wanted a private tour of the place. Did anyone else get the same invitation?"

Shaking heads and mumbles of, "Nope, not me," surfaced as Allie gave a knowing but uncomfortable smile to the table as she averted her eyes and felt heat flush her face.

"Trust me, Allie from LA," Linda said, "if that gorgeous butch asked me to join her on a private tour of the island, you'd be finding interesting-looking designs in the sand come morning." She elbowed Allie. "Know what I mean?"

"I'm pretty sure I know what you mean," Allie said through a forced smile. She wasn't here for a hookup and she didn't need to—according to Reba—get some playtime in so she could grease her rusty parts. But if she was being totally honest with herself, there was another reason she wasn't interested in Jo. And that reason resided in the house just up the cove from where she was dining.

"Catch her, Jo!" A scratchy voice shouted in between profanities, interrupting Allie's thoughts as a pig with an apple in her mouth came trotting through the area. "Get her!" A short, stout, elderly woman with long silver hair and deep lines etched in her dark brown skin, waved a wooden spoon over her head as she limped behind, cursing up a storm.

Jo chuckled as the pig ran by her. "Here we go again. Mila, you know I'm not about to wrestle food away from Gizmo." Jo placed an arm around Mila's shoulders, stopping her in her tracks. "Come on, I'm sure there're plenty of other apples in your kitchen."

Mila shrugged away from Jo's arm and smacked her on the shoulder with the wooden spoon. "That damn pig knocked over the entire bowl. And those were my pie baking apples. Kate needs to keep her on a leash."

"I'll let Kate know Gizzy got in your kitchen…again." Jo's tone was calming. "Meanwhile." She stopped in front of the table. "Allie, meet Mila, the resort's chef extraordinaire."

Allie stood and extended her arm. "It's a pleasure to meet you. I think your cooking is extraordinary, and I would love to know what your secret spices and sauces consist of."

Mila glanced at Allie's outstretched hand, huffed, and gave her a not so subtle once over as she turned to Jo, smacked her again with the spoon, and hobbled away while grumbling. Jo stood laughing as she rubbed her arm.

"You're right, she's feisty." Allie said as they stood watching Mila limp away.

"Told ya. But I could tell she took your compliment to heart."

"You could tell that by her grunt?"

"Yeah, that's more than she gives most people when she first meets them. She likes you."

"Wow, okay, if you say so."

"I do."

"What's going to happen to the pig?" Allie said with concern. When she was in junior high school, a classmate had brought his pet potbellied pig to a school function. She'd fallen in love and over dinner that evening had begged her parents to let her adopt a pig. Her mother had reacted by reaching over and feeling her forehead to see if she had a fever, and her dad had just sat there eating while giving her his signature look of disgust. The topic was put to rest without either of them uttering a single word.

"Are you kidding? First of all, Gizmo is never in trouble. That pig is Kate's pride and joy and has the run of this place. And secondly, don't let Mila fool you. She loves Giz as much as Kate does. I've caught her several times sitting on the beach late at night with Gizmo by her side. Just the two of them. And Mila feeds her bowls of scraps while talking her ear off. Besides, if Mila really wanted Gizmo out of her kitchen, all she would have to do is shut the door. I'm telling you, it's a dance between those two."

Allie nodded. "Gotcha."

"But be warned, Gizmo is a bit of a kleptomaniac, so if you find that you're missing any personal items, she's probably the culprit."

"I'll have to remember that."

"So..." Jo's voice was low. "See you after dessert?"

"Actually, I don't think I can eat another bite." She rubbed her extended belly, not remembering the last time she'd eaten to the point of uncomfortableness because the taste of the food was that addictive.

"Oh?" Jo arched a brow. "In that case, would you like to walk it off?"

Allie heard throats being cleared and saw nods of encouragement from the women at the table. "Um, sure. Yeah, why not?"

Jo extended her hand, and as Allie wrapped her fingers around hers, she was keenly aware that no sparks went off and no butterflies ran laps around her stomach. And if there was even the slightest doubt as to who had captured her body's attention on this island, this was confirmation. Still, what woman didn't appreciate being swooned over every once in a while?

CHAPTER SIX

K ate kept the binoculars pressed to her eyes as she fumbled to hit the speaker icon on her phone. "Yeah?"

"Hey, boss, calling you back."

"Carla," Kate said as she watched Jo extend a hand toward Allie and escort her away from the dining table. "Do me a favor. Keep close tabs on our guest in Casita Four and let me know the minute she goes out on her boat. She promised me she wasn't a treasure hunter, but I still don't trust her." Kate had done a quick social media search on Allie, and after visiting three sites, she had a pretty good idea about who the only other woman who had taken her breath away was. And although none of the photos or posts mentioned anything about treasure hunting, she couldn't deny the circumstantial evidence and the feeling of dread in her gut.

"Will do. Anything else?"

"No, that's all. Thanks, Carla."

"Sure thing, boss," Carla said as the line went dead.

Kate continued to watch as Allie entwined her hand in Jo's and was led away from the table in the direction of the beach. "What am I going to do with you, Jo?" She lowered the binoculars from her face and tapped the lens in thought. She had heard the stories of Jo hooking up with a couple of guests, and she had told her that as long as it was consensual and didn't create drama for the other guests or the resort, she was okay with it. This was, after all, a place for adult women, and if one or two wanted a tropical tryst while staying here, who was she to deny that pleasure? Jo was a charmer, and the single ladies seemed to respond well to her.

Hmm, this never bothered her before, so why this time? She folded into her lounge chair and couldn't deny the twinge of jealousy tugging at her emotions. "Get a grip," she scolded herself for the schoolgirl crush. Besides, how ridiculous was it to think that after a brief encounter, she could actually be developing feelings for someone? She scoffed at the thought as Gizmo came grunting onto the porch. She jumped into the chair beside Kate and began munching on something.

"Whatchca got there, Giz?" Kate cocked her head. "Uh-oh, Mila's going to tan your hide one of these days if you keep stealing from her kitchen." Kate lightheartedly laughed as she patted Gizmo's head, then trained her eyes on the ocean. She pressed into the cushion and watched the glint of the moon dance across the surface of the water. She took a couple of deep breaths when she noticed she was still a bit on edge and glanced again at the binoculars as she fought the urge to use them to spy on Allie and Jo.

Wow, what's that about? She had only used her binoculars to look out over the ocean when she'd caught glimpses of aquatic life. She took another breath as the answer to her lingering thoughts surfaced. "Allie," she whispered at the image of the woman with smooth, light brown skin; shoulder-length black hair; and light golden-brown eyes that sparkled with each smile. Only once before had her body reacted so strongly when meeting a woman. And that person became her heart, soul, and breath. When she'd died, she'd taken a part of Kate with her, including what she'd thought was the ability to ever be attracted to anyone. And now, a treasure hunter from her old hometown showed up, and those feelings she'd thought were reserved for just one had resurfaced. She felt it the moment Allie had opened the door. Kate closed her eyes as the slight breeze from the ocean covered her and cooled her thoughts. What the actual hell?

❖

Startled from the jingle of her phone, Kate fumbled for the device as she tried to clear her head. "Yeah," she grumbled as she wiped the sleep from her eyes and squinted at the rising sun. She had once again fallen asleep on the lounge chair under the comfortable blanket of stars. Not the worst habit she had ever had.

"Sorry to bother you, boss, but you wanted me to notify you when Casita Four was on the move. Well, she's heading toward the dock right now."

"Thanks, Carla. I appreciate you notifying me."

"Sure thing, boss, anything else?"

"No...oh wait, yes. When you get a chance, could you bring up a bowl of scraps for Gizmo?" She flopped her head to her side and smiled as Gizmo sprawled out on the lounge chair next to her, snoring. "And please apologize to Mila regarding Gizzy's behavior last night. I noticed she stole another apple."

"Will do."

"Thanks, Carla." She stood, stretched, grabbed her binoculars off the table, and searched the dock for Allie. "Let's see what you're up to this morning," she said as she spotted her hopping in her boat. Allie was wearing board shorts and a bikini top, and a backpack was slung over her shoulder. Kate licked her lips as a slight tingle presented itself in her stomach. She wondered if she and Jo had hooked up last night, and that thought brought on more unexpected feelings. So what if they had? It was none of her business. And yet, the very fact that she was thinking about it meant that she was making it her business.

She shook the thoughts from her head as she refocused on Allie. Huh, she grunted to herself. Years ago, when she was partying her way through the women of LA, she would have never given someone so wholesome-looking a second thought. Funny how sobriety cleared her vison so she could see her herself, and others, through different eyes.

She watched the boat head due east, then stop approximately two hundred yards out. "What are you doing out there, Allie?" She refocused the long-range lenses. She needed to know if her hunch was right as she gazed at Allie shrugging on her scuba gear, throwing a diver down flag in the water and hiking one leg onto the side of the boat as she strapped a knife to her calf. Kate admired her lean muscle tone as she twisted her leg from side to side, obviously checking the position of the blade. Damn. The scenery was definitely grabbing her attention. A butterfly took a lap around her stomach as she focused on Allie's lips gliding over the regulator's mouthpiece as she placed it in her mouth and…

"Hey, boss."

Kate jerked, dropped the binoculars, and made a spectacular save right before they hit the marble floor. "Holy hell, Carla, you scared the shit out of me. How about knocking next time?"

"Knock? When have I ever knocked?" Carla placed a bowl of chopped veggies on the ground and cooed to Gizmo. "Hey, Gizzy girl, breakfast."

Gizmo opened her eyes, jumped off the lounge chair, and grunted a greeting as her tail swished back and forth. Carla bent, rubbed her under her chin, and kissed her head. "There you go, girl. Now then." She stood and faced Kate. "I'll let you get back to your spying."

"I wasn't spying."

"Uh-huh."

"Okay, maybe a little."

"Is this gonna be a new hobby of yours, or are we talking just while Allie is on the island?"

Kate handed Carla the binoculars. "She's getting ready to dive, and I wanted to see if she was going down with the metal detector."

Carla moved the binoculars in a sweeping motion. "I don't see her anywhere." She handed them back to Kate.

"Shit, she already jumped in." Kate scanned the area, then turned to Carla. "Tell me something, Carla. If you were a recreational diver, where would you dive?"

Carla paused for a moment before answering. "I'd go to the wrecks or stay in the cove where the sea life is abundant and the chances of encountering turtles and rays is high."

"Exactly. Out where she is, she'll see, what…a fraction of the sea life? Why not just dive in the spectacular areas the Bahamas are known for?"

Carla shrugged. "Don't know."

"Because she's a treasure hunter. There's no other explanation. She's not diving to see the sights. She's diving out there for another reason." She should just throw Allie off the island for defying her request, and yet, she couldn't help being drawn to someone so mysterious and alluring. Ever since they'd shaken hands and that momentary contact had reignited feelings she hasn't had snice Brooke, Kate hadn't been able to get Allie out of her mind. Damn, she had never been so conflicted in wanting to push someone away and bring them close.

"Uh-oh, I know that look. Things are going to start to get weird, aren't they?" Carla pointed an accusatory finger at her.

"Carla?" Kate turned. "You still know your way around a boat motor, don't you?"

"I know my way around a car motor, but I doubt they're that much different…why?"

"Oh, I was just thinking how unfortunate it would be if Allie's boat suffered a mechanical complication that grounded it for the remainder of her stay." It seemed the best compromise to her conflicting feelings was to get rid of the treasure hunting while not getting rid of the treasure hunter.

"You want me to tamper with her boat?"

"Just the motor and nothing that can't be easily reversed. You know, like a hose or belt thingy that just *happened* to fall off."

"A hose or belt thingy?"

"Well, whatever boat motors use to make them run. Besides, just look at that thing." Kate motioned with a tilt of her head. "She would never suspect anything if she came out tomorrow morning, and it wouldn't start."

"We've devolved into sabotage, have we?" Carla displayed a twinge of nervousness in her voice and expression.

Kate slumped back in her lounge chair. "I just don't want to deal with the attention if she finds anything. Look how close to the cay she's hunting. If there's even a hint of treasure, boats from all over will be anchored out there. I know the ocean isn't private property, but this cay is, and I'd like to keep the emphasis on the word *private* as much as possible. For myself as much as the guests." But mostly for herself.

"Why not just throw her off the island? It isn't like you haven't done that before."

"Because I, um," she stammered as she hesitated about confiding her feelings. To let Carla know that last night was the first night in years that she'd fallen asleep with a woman besides Brooke on her mind? Yes, she should be able to say all of that to Carla, and yet, she thought if she verbally confirmed her attraction, it would feel as though she was cheating on Brooke. "Just because, okay?"

Kate could see the wheels spin in Carla's head as a smile tugged at the corners of her mouth. "When do you want me to do this?"

"Tonight, when everyone's asleep."

Carla nodded. "For the record, I totally disagree with all of this, but since you're the boss—"

"Yes, I am, and thank you, Carla." Kate cut her off because she knew she was asking something that, deep down, she was a little uncomfortable with. But for the privacy of the resort, she justified her request. "I'll make it up to you, I promise. Meanwhile, I think I'll take Gertrude out and go pay Allie a little visit."

"You're taking Gertrude out?" The shock in Carla's voice didn't go unnoticed.

Gertrude was one of the names Brooke had given to their matching pair of Jet Skis named after two mermaid characters from her favorite childhood book. Gertrude was Kate's, and Gretta was Brooke's, and she hadn't taken either out since Brooke had died. It was just one of those memories she avoided revisiting.

"Yes," was all Kate felt like saying, hoping the single word would suffice and end the topic. The moment of silence between them seemed to convey it had done just that.

"Well," Carla said. "I best be going."

"How are the guests settling in?"

"Great. They're a fun group. The honeymooners stayed in their casita all evening, but they have a ten o'clock paddleboard lesson booked with Jo after breakfast. We'll see if they show up for either. My bet is they don't. And the gang from Canada is going snorkeling with Julie, except one, who's staying landbound."

Kate knew her crew would keep the aquatic activities restricted to the lagoon. The water was calm, clear, and shallow enough to be safe. As a bonus, several turtles and rays hung out on a daily basis, which were always a treat for the guests. Of course, the snorkeling by her end of the island was much more spectacular, but she wanted to be respectful of Bruce's space, as well as the liability of having guests swimming in an area known to have a shark in it. Even though Bruce seemed totally harmless, he was still a shark, and people still did dumb things, and the combination meant that area was off-limits.

"You joining any of the activities?"

Carla shook her head. "I'm going to see if Mila needs help in the kitchen today."

"Wait…what?" Kate's mind came to a screeching halt. Mila had always made it crystal clear that no one was ever allowed in her kitchen. Ever. The fact that Carla was going to help her meant something was up. "What happened? What's wrong?" she said with concern.

"Calm down, nothing happened." Carla waved her off. "I've just noticed something's a little off with her lately. Maybe it's the pain in her hands. I can tell her arthritis is getting worse. I can see it. Things like chopping must be more difficult for her, even though she'd be the last to admit it. I figured I'd just walk in unannounced and see if she'd let me help her out."

"You know she's going to whup your ass with that spoon of hers the moment you set foot in there."

"Well, it won't be the first time I've had an ass whupping."

"That's nice of you. You think one of these days, she'll let me hire her an assistant?"

Carla snorted. "Over her dead body. We're talking about Mila here. She's more stubborn than a mule."

"That she is." Kate stood, stretched, and grabbed her polarized aviator sunglasses off the table. "Okay, I'm heading out to see what Allie's really doing out there."

"Uh-huh." Carla's tone seemed uncaring as she flopped on the lounge chair and focused on her phone.

Kate paused before leaving as she patted Gizmo on the head and softened her voice. "I'll be right back. Meanwhile, hang out here with Aunt Carla." She snatched the Rainbow's End T-shirt that had been draped over the back of the chair for God only knew how long and scurried down the path toward the beach. "Make yourself at home while I'm gone," she called over her shoulder.

"I always do."

Kate jogged to the small floating dock she had constructed close to her house. The two Jet Skis, hers purple and Brooke's cherry red, were sitting out of the water, and as she peeled back Gertrude's cover, her breath caught as a wave of emotions crashed into her. The Skis were their one-year wedding anniversary presents to themselves, and although she had Jo make sure they were maintained properly, she had not taken either out since Brooke had died. She exhaled a breath laced with sadness as she opened the small lockbox, grabbed the spiral cord under the small plastic etched sign designating it as Gertrude's, approached the Ski, and slowly swung her leg over the machine. She settled into the seat and took a moment to glide her hands gently over the handlebars as though she was reacquainting herself with a long-lost friend. "It's been a while, huh, old girl?" She inserted the key that was dangling from the cord in the ignition and clipped the other end to her shorts.

"Last one on the water cooks dinner tonight." She heard Brooke's voice in her head as she glanced at Gretta. A vision of Brooke straddling the Ski was smiling back at her through windblown hair. "Ready, babe?"

"Ready." Kate stood on the tips of her toes and rapidly backed the Ski off the dock ramp and into the ocean. "Ha, beat ya," she said as she bobbed in the water and glanced over her shoulder at no one. She gazed back at the dock where Gretta was still sitting, covered and untouched. She scrubbed her hands through her hair and exhaled a shaky breath as she hit the ignition button. Maybe it was time to give the Jet Ski to someone who'd love it as much as Brooke had. There was something sad and pathetic seeing it sitting there looking as lonely as she felt. After taking another breath to stabilize her thoughts, she squeezed the throttle and turned her attention away from Gretta and toward Allie.

She zigzagged out to Allie's boat, taking time to hop several waves and do a few doughnuts. She had forgotten how invigorating it was being back on the Ski. By the time she slowed and maneuvered Gertrude next to Allie's boat, she was drenched and sporting a smile that stretched her cheeks. "Ahoy, there."

No answer.

"Allie?" She craned her neck and glanced in the boat. It was empty. A moment of anxiety punched at her stomach as her mind shifted to worry. Allie had been down there awhile, and tiger sharks were known to frequent these waters. She shaded her eyes and scanned the area. A few minutes later, she noticed a cluster of bubbles heading her way. She cut her engine, grabbed the side of the boat, and anchored herself.

Allie surfaced about twenty yards out, removed her regulator, and pushed the mask onto her forehead. She used her hand to squeegee water off her face, then rolled over and back kicked to the boat. Kate focused on Allie's breasts, now above the water, the blue bikini material wet and clinging to her skin. Her nipples were so erect they looked as though they were about to poke through the fabric. As Allie approached the boat, she rolled her upper body back into the water and grabbed the ladder.

"Ahoy, there."

Allie jerked. "Oh my God, Kate, you startled me. What are you doing here?" She hooked one arm around the aluminum ladder, took her fins off, and tossed them onto the deck.

"I was in the neighborhood, so I figured I'd stop by and say hi."

"Well, how nice." Allie grabbed the sides of the ladder and stepped into the boat.

At that point, Kate should have offered to help her out of her scuba gear, but as the water snaked down Allie's body, and her muscles flexed in a tantalizing way as she shrugged out of the tank, Kate was finding it hard to concentrate on words, much less actions.

"How, um," she stumbled as Allie freed herself from her mask, cocked her leg up on the side of the boat, and unclipped the strap that had fastened the knife and sheath to her calf.

"There." Allie's words snapped Kate out of her lustful trance. "That feels better."

"How, um." Kate cleared her throat and thoughts. "How was it down there?"

"Nice. The water's warm, and the visibility is exceptional. I'm so used to diving in the murky waters off Long Beach that this is quite a treat."

"Best diving waters anywhere or so the Bahama tourism office likes to brag."

"Well." Allie tilted her upper body and squeezed some water out of her hair. "I think they're right." She smiled. "Hey, why don't you tie your Ski up and join me. I was thinking about having some breakfast, and I know you're just dying to come aboard and check out this marvel of a vessel." She waved her hands and referenced her surroundings.

Kate popped open the front holding compart on the Ski, retrieved a rope, and tied Gertrude to the boat's cleat. "Funny,

I was just thinking the other day how incomplete my life has been because I have yet to have breakfast on a boat that—"

"Looks like it's held together with duct tape and a prayer?" Allie asked. "Trust me when I say it's a long story." She extended her arm.

Kate hooked her fingers around Allie's hand and in one motion, hopped on board and steadied herself inches from her. They stood, fingers still entwined as they gazed into each other's eyes. Water droplets still clung to Allie's light brown skin, and as Kate caught a whiff of saltwater mixed with the slightest hint of coconut sunscreen, goose bumps flashed over her, carrying with it a tingle of unexpected desire. She wanted to close the short distance between them, cup Allie's face, and let their tongues do a dance that would prep their bodies for something more substantial.

"We, uh." Allie licked her lips. "We could hold on the breakfast Jo packed until later."

And there it was, like the sound of a needle scratching across a vinyl record, bringing with it the one word that cooled her desire. Jo. Ah yes, the two of them seemed to have already hit it off, and that caused a bit of bile to scorch the back of her throat as she took a step back. "No. You've been in the water all morning. You must be hungry. We should eat," she said in a dry tone as she leaned against the side of the boat.

"Oh, yes, of course," Allie said as she retreated and in a scattered movement, retrieved a canvas bag.

"We've got banana nut bread and some cut fruit." Allie displayed small plastic containers as she glanced around. "Sorry, no chairs. I hope you're up for picnic style?" She plopped down, crossed her legs, flattened the bag, and placed the containers of food on top.

"My kind of dining." Kate sat opposite her and grabbed a slice of bread. "Did you see anything exciting down there?"

"Not really. A bunch of parrot fish, some angels, a few schools of other silver fish I didn't recognize, and a curious eel that hung out with me for a few moments before moving on. I'll tell you one thing, though, it feels good to be back in the water. It's been a while."

"Oh yeah? How long?"

"Well." she cocked her head in thought. "It's been just over four years. Shelly, my ex, was a co-owner of a dive shop in Long Beach. She introduced me to the wonders of the hobby and taught me everything I know. Unfortunately, after the breakup, I stopped diving."

"Why?"

"Well, for starters, it's expensive when you're no longer getting the perks of sleeping with one of the owners, and secondly, my dad was starting to have health issues, and I was spending more and more time at the restaurant." She glanced at Kate. "Our place is called Aukai's Family Diner. It's in east LA. I'm sure you've heard of it," she said in a playful way.

"Hmm, can't say the name rings a bell," Kate replied with as much playfulness.

"Well, aren't you missing out? Our claim to fame is a special cheese sauce that's served with every meal, and trust me when I say there's nothing special about it. My dad just called it that, and since most of our clientele are so old that they can't taste much anymore, they just take our word for it. Nothing like Mila's cooking. This banana nut bread is delicious, and last night's meal was outstanding."

"Before Mila came to the resort, her specialty was everything conch. Conch stew, conch fritters, conch salad, cracked conch, and conch ceviche. When I told her I wanted the resort to be meat free, she told me I had the wrong chef. All her family recipes called for conch. It took a while, and a few failed attempts, but now, her food always gets five-star reviews from the guests." She took a moment to flick a grape in her mouth as she reflected on the little shack on Nassau that had seemed to attract a long line of people waiting to be served. She had noticed the place one day when she was there picking up some supplies and had thought, if it drew that much of a crowd, there must be something about the food that was worth the wait. So she'd found a place in line and almost thirty minutes later was sitting on the ground dipping a conch fritter into a sauce cup. The combined taste came alive in her mouth, and by her third bite, she found herself offering the crotchety old woman in the shack a job as chef of her resort. Mila's first words were for Kate to piss off, followed by a long breath of mostly unrecognizable words that were easily interpreted by her gestures.

Several weeks later, when Kate had returned to Nassau, she'd noticed the shack was vacant. She'd asked some of the locals about it and was told that Mila had been robbed and the shack vandalized. She'd then inquired as to where Mila lived and was pointed in the direction of an area about a twenty-minute walk that had a known reputation of being a bit on the sketchy side. When Kate had approached a house that looked as run-down as the food shack, she'd seen Mila sitting on the top of two rotted wooden steps.

Kate had kept a respectable distance as she'd told Mila she had heard what had happened with her food shack and doubled her original offer to come work at the resort. Mila had sat silently, staring with a faraway gaze, never once acknowledging Kate's presence. After almost thirty minutes of trying to get Mila to engage in conversation, Kate had conceded defeat and as she'd turned to walk away, she'd heard the barely audible word that would change both their lives: okay.

"Think Mila would ever give up her recipes?" Allie's words brought Kate back to the present. "If I had her talents, I think I could really turn my parents' diner around."

"You'd have a better chance wrestling a meal away from a bull shark." Kate kept her tone matter-of-fact.

Allie chuckled. "Yeah, I saw a bit of her feistiness last night when she was chasing Gizmo over an apple."

"Yes, Giz does seem to have a stubborn tendency to believe that what's yours is really hers. But don't let Mila fool you. She and Gizmo are the best of buddies."

"So I've heard."

They fell into a comfortable silence, and as Allie lowered her gaze and grabbed another slice of bread, Kate took advantage of the moment and studied her. She was sweet, had a smile that could light up a room, and seemed to have an innocence about her that Kate found charmingly attractive. She felt the need to get to know her likes and dislikes, what she did for fun, and all the little intricacies of her life, when the corner of her eye caught the tip of the metal detector hanging out of the bin, and all the warm fuzzy feelings were trampled as she was reminded why she was there. "Please tell me you're not planning on using that thing to go treasure hunting."

"What?" Allie followed her line of sight. "Oh, no…no, I'm not. It came with—"

Kate saw Allie's lips move, but all she could hear was her own voice telling her she was being played. "Allie, I meant it when I said it's a resort policy."

"Kate, I'm not a treasure hunter, that was just part of a—"

"Because if you really are just a recreational diver as you say, could you please explain the metal detector?" She sensed by Allie's stiff body language that her tone was a bit more accusatory than she had intended. But damn it, she was not going to tolerate being lied to. She'd spent her entire childhood being hurt by those who'd practiced the art of deception and dodging accountability with statements like, it was only a white lie, it was for your own good that we didn't tell you the truth, you're too young to understand; or the all-time classic, you misunderstood. Excuses were just a way for the liar to justify their actions. And by the time she'd hit double-digit years, she'd too become a master at the game. All taught to her courtesy of good ol' Mom and Dad.

Brooke was the first to see through her veil of lies and hold her accountable. Carla was the second. So as she sat facing Allie, looking for the telltale sign of a flinch or twitch that contradicted whatever statement Allie was about to hand her, Kate had to admit, nothing about Allie's vibe was pinging her bullshit meter. Still.

"Wow, where did that come from? And you do realize you totally cut me off twice when I was *trying* to explain while you continued to accuse me of being something I'm not." Allie said as she glanced away and shook her head. "And you know what else I'm not?" She turned back and squared off with Kate. "I'm not a liar." Her tone was defensive and layered with what Kate perceived as total disgust. "And right now, I think maybe you should go."

The words felt like a slap to Kate, as did the look of hurt in Allie's eyes. She hopped to her feet as conflicting feelings surfaced. Half of her wanted to apologize for not trusting Allie, and the other half held firm that her assumption was correct. Was it true that Allie had a right to do whatever she wanted in public waters? Yes. Yes, she did. But in Kate's eyes, that privilege ended at the point where it could potentially affect the resort and of course, her.

"Allie, I…" Kate wanted to explain why it meant so much to her to keep the waters around the cay private. That Allie had no idea what it was like to have one's privacy stripped away because—as she was told more than once while growing up—that was just part of the deal. Then, to finally feel, for the first time in her life, the freedom of living with anonymity. It was a feeling she'd do almost anything to maintain.

Allie held up an interrupting hand. "Don't. Please, just go."

"Allie?" She took a step in her direction.

"Please."

"Fine." Kate huffed under her breath as she pushed her sunglasses farther up her nose, hopped on Gertrude, and started the engine.

"Fine," Allie snapped back.

Kate revved the accelerator, glanced one more time at Allie, and sped off, spraying water in her wake. She felt the tears begin to well in her eyes as the Ski hopped across the water. Wow, what had brought those on? She did a quick mental tally, and the list was long. Regret over her bitchiness. Frustration over newly realized feelings of jealousy with Jo. Childhood issues yet unresolved from therapy. Or were they tears of anger over Allie's overt defiance and dismissiveness of her request?

"Fuck," she yelled over the noise of the Ski as she eased back on the accelerator that she had been white-knuckling on full throttle. Maybe she should have listened when Allie was trying to explain herself and not had such a knee-jerk reaction. After all, Allie had not been a part of the dysfunction that had shaped Kate's world. But right now, the ghosts of her past were toying with her judgment, and they were telling her Allie was a threat to a lifestyle she would defend at all costs.

She powered down her Ski and as she bobbed in the water, calmed her breath and heart rate, took her sunglasses off, and wiped her face on the sleeve of her T-shirt. When she placed her glasses back on, her Ski had drifted a one-eighty in its position. She took a moment to refocus on Allie's boat but couldn't see her anywhere. She exhaled long and slow. The evidence was undeniable, but maybe Allie deserved the one thing Kate had the hardest time giving: trust.

But old feelings were hard to change and so were old habits. Stubbornness and self-preservation at all costs were Bennett family traits, and she had been told more than once that her apple hadn't fallen far from that tree.

CHAPTER SEVEN

"Wow, that went south fast." Allie shook off the water that had sprayed her as Kate had sped away. Maybe she should have been more forceful when it came to explaining herself, but really? Should she have had to? She was in public waters, two-hundred yards from the resort, trying to find a spot to bury her dad, and Kate had the audacity to call her a liar.

"*Fuck.*" She let lose a primal scream that she'd learned in therapy, kicked at the metal detector, then hopped in a small circle trying to curb the pain now throbbing in her big toe. "Shit, shit, shit," she grumbled as her phone jingled. She hobbled to her backpack, took a couple of deep breaths, and swiped her finger across the screen. "Hey, Reba."

"Uh-oh, you don't sound too good."

"Oh, it's nothing. I just stubbed my toe on the equipment bin. What's up?" She tried to rub the pain away as she scrunched her face in agony.

"I'm calling because as you know, I have no patience. Did you bury your dad?"

"No. He's back at the casita. I decided to spend the day diving in the area and just get a feel for what it looks like. I think I found a spot by a cluster of small boulders that'll work. I'll come out again first thing in the morning, do a little ritual, bury his urn, and that'll be that. Then, I'll spend the rest of my time here enjoying what the resort has to offer." And try to avoid Kate, and her feelings for her, as much as possible.

"And the women, don't forget about what the women have to offer."

Allie rolled her eyes. She was getting a little annoyed at Reba's constant insistence that she find a hookup while she was here. "Well, it just so happens that the mysterious Kate Williams was on my boat."

"You have my undivided attention."

"There's nothing to tell. She was out on her Jet Ski and came over to see what I was doing. We shared some banana nut bread and fruit and..." Allie heard snoring sounds coming from her phone. "Stop that." She wasn't in the mood for Reba's antics right now.

"Sorry, but I mean, come on. You've never been on a real vacation, you're in the Bahamas at a women's resort, a beautiful woman was just on your boat, and you're giving me the play-by-play as though you're reading off a grocery list. Was she at least cool with you burying your dad?"

"I didn't tell her, and now she thinks I'm a treasure hunter."

"A treasure hunter? Why would she think that?"

"Because a metal detector came as part of the scuba gear package as their promotional special this month. She saw it, made the assumption, then called me a liar when I told her I wasn't."

"Oh wow. That's not cool. Did you clarify it with her?"

"I tried, but she kept cutting me off. She just..." Allie stumbled as she tried to free the lump in her throat. "She just..." Tears dripped down her cheeks as she squinted across the water and focused on nothing.

"Allie?"

"I, um." She took a couple deep breaths and fanned her face. "Wow, don't know what came over me just then. Sorry about that." Was the sudden release of emotion more about her dad or Kate? Or was being back in the water for the first time since Shelly bringing something up? She had been tamping down feelings of loneliness the past few years, and maybe the ocean was reminding her, in that therapeutic way it did, how empty her life felt lately.

She had Reba, of course, and a handful of other friends that she could call and hang with whenever she wanted. Her mom was still around, and the regulars at the restaurant felt like uncles and aunts, so the loneliness wasn't from any of the above parts of her life not being fulfilled. No, this feeling was coming from deep within her heart. That part of the muscle that only beat when a certain someone jump-started it. She hadn't felt *that* feeling in a very long time. No, scratch that, she hadn't felt that feeling since yesterday when she'd opened the door to Kate.

She filled her lungs as a slight ocean breeze blew over her. Being alone and being lonely were two very different feelings, and right now, the latter of the two was starting to hurt.

"Hey." Reba's voice was soothing. "You've been through a lot in your life, especially lately. You have a right to a good cry or ten. Hell, when you think about it, it's kinda amazing you turned out as normal as you did."

"Gee, thanks." Allie snorted, even though the comment made her smile.

"Kidding. But seriously, let whatever you're feeling come out, but don't let it ruin your time there. This week is all about you."

"Thanks, Reba." Maybe that was another reason for her tears. It felt good being away from her reality. Although she naturally worried about her mom, not having the daily tether of the diner shackling her was a taste of freedom she couldn't remember ever feeling, and the selfish part of her didn't want to give that up.

"All right, in the meantime, forget about Kate, have fun, and send more pics. And not of the ocean at sunset. I know what that looks like, for fuck's sake, we live in LA."

"Okay. More pics of things besides the sunset, got it."

"Yeah, like maybe that cute butch you mentioned yesterday. Send a pic of her. I could use some eye candy right about now."

"Thought you had a date with the lead actress this weekend. Why not just take a pic of her?"

Silence.

"Oh, Reba." Acknowledgment hit her as she softened her tone. "I'm so sorry. What happened?" She had told Reba more than once to stop falling for the actresses she worked with because the relationships always seemed to end when the film wrapped.

"Seems as though she hooked up with the producer. Guess she had more to offer her than I did."

"Hey, stop that. You are an amazing woman, beautiful, funny as hell, intelligent, and the best makeup artist in Hollywood. Screw her for not seeing that in you."

"Thanks, Allie, you too. Well, you know, not the makeup part and all, but the rest is also true for you. Screw Kate for not seeing that in you."

Allie smiled and wondered how many times she and Reba had picked up the shattered pieces of the other's expectations and helped put them back together.

"Hey, I gotta go, they're calling me on set. Get this, the girlfriend-stealing producer decided it wasn't in the budget to hire any more extras, so they're using cardboard people for the background, and she wants me to touch them up and make them look more real. I'm telling ya, you can't make this shit up. Anyway, love you." Allie heard the smack of a kiss. "Now go get laid. It'll make you feel better."

"Stop already," Allie said lightheartedly as she disconnected and tapped the phone against her thigh in thought as Reba's words echoed in her head. Maybe she should take Jo up on her offer. Reba was right: this was a once-in-a-lifetime vacation for her and would probably be her last time away from the restaurant until her mom passed. The *fuck it* side of her wanted to forget about Kate, run into Jo's arms, and for the next several days, have one hell of a distracted fling.

But the other side of her, the side that listened to her heart, was saying no. Besides, casual hookups had never been her thing. She reactivated her phone and against her better judgment, typed in Suzanne Bennett. The search brought her to the same places she had already been until her eye caught a link from a publication out of the UK that had a picture of Kate smiling, her arms around a woman.

"Brooke Monroe," Allie whispered as she read the headline under the semi-blurry picture, "is rumored to be the latest in a string of girlfriends for the heiress, Suzanne Bennett." The woman looked a little older and unlike the other girlfriends Kate was photographed with, wasn't flashy, runway model thin, or dressed like a Hollywood movie star. Instead, Brooke was curvy; had fire-red, shoulder-length hair; wore a vintage style dress; and sported a smile that instantly drew one in. She reminded Allie of her eighth-grade algebra teacher and first crush. The article stated that they were rumored to be taking up residence at the family's Bahamas' cay.

Huh. Allie was sure Kate was single. At least, that was the vibe she got from her. "What happened to you two?" She wondered as she did several more searches for Brooke Monroe until she stumbled upon a small article about a posthumous dedication of a new wing for a gay youth homeless shelter that was named after Brooke. There was no accompanying photo, but if that was the same Brooke Monroe, that would answer some of her lingering questions around Kate.

Allie tossed her phone on her backpack, shoved another bite of banana bread in her mouth, and was relieved that the pain in her toe had subsided, and the digit seemed functional again. She shrugged into another tank, grabbed her mask and fins, and jumped in.

As she slowly descended to the sandy bottom, enjoying the peaceful Zen that the weightlessness of the water provided, some of the air bubbles brushed her cheeks, and she briefly thought again about her ex, Shelly. Their relationship had been dysfunctional and tumultuous, but she would be forever grateful to her for introducing her to this world full of magic and beauty. Where colorful and mesmerizing inhabitants resembled mystical beings, and where the environment rejuvenated instead of drained her.

She located the small clusters of rocks she had singled out as a good spot to bury her dad's urn and took a moment to settle next to them on bent knees as a plume of sand kicked up around her and sparkled as the particles caught a sunbeam before floating back down. She slowed her breathing and tried to become one with the serenity of the ocean. She closed her eyes and intermittently held her breath so she could enjoy the silence without the echoing sound of her breath through her regulator.

She settled into a meditative state, tried to clear her mind, but couldn't quite get the last thoughts of Kate out of her head. She was undeniably attracted to Kate; that was evident from her body's reaction every time she saw her. But the chances of anything developing from those feelings was zero to none, especially after what had just happened. She tilted her head from shoulder to shoulder and tried again to calm her mind, but it was clear that thoughts of Kate were not going to release their grip, and that was troubling. She didn't want to be obsessed with someone who had not only accused her of being a liar but didn't respect her enough to hear her out. She was done trying to prove herself to someone who didn't seem to care.

She opened her eyes and glanced around to take inventory of her surroundings, hoping to distract herself with the ocean's inhabitants. A turtle and several schools of fish swam above her, seemingly unfazed by her presence. She admired their grace and ease as they glided through the water, and she was reminded again that she was just a visitor in their world.

She kicked off the rocks and slowly headed in the opposite direction of the boat and farther out to sea when a glimmer of something gold in the sand caught her eye. As she approached the unidentifiable object, she thought about Kate's obvious animosity toward treasure hunting and her promise that she wasn't here to unearth relics from the past, but she couldn't help the twinge of excitement that surged through her body as she briskly fanned her hand over the area. Through the haze of the disturbed sediment, she saw an outline of something round and plunged her fingers in after it. A flash of a car she had been wanting to buy but couldn't afford danced in her head. She decided at that moment that if what she'd found truly was a treasure, she would keep it a secret until she got back home to cash it in, and even then, never disclose the location of her find.

Her heart pounded, and her eyes widened in anticipation as she slowly opened her hand and let the sand rapidly drain from her fingers, exposing the artifact. She blew out a burst of bubbles that carried her laughter to the surface as she slipped the gold-plated Timex watch on her wrist. Her dad's words echoed in her head: "There's no such thing as free money." She continued to chuckle in her regulator as she ventured farther into the vastness of the ocean and reminded herself that the only true treasure out here was the beauty of her surroundings.

Four hours later, she was waving at Jo, who stood on the dock waiting for her return. "Ahoy there, Allie!" Jo waved.

"Ahoy there, Jo." She threw the rope out to her, and Jo tied her up.

Jo held out a helping hand. "Did you have a nice time diving?"

"I did." She shrugged on her backpack and grabbed Jo's extended hand as she stepped off the boat. "And I even found a little treasure while out there." She displayed and rotated her wrist.

"Wow, that's quite the relic. We get stuff like that washing up onshore from time to time, but lately, it's been nothing but old beer cans. Anyway." Jo flanked Allie as they headed back to the resort. "I'm glad you enjoyed your dive."

"Yes, and thank you for packing breakfast. It was delicious. Kate was even out Jet Skiing and stopped by for a few minutes, so I shared some of the—"

"Kate was out with Gertrude? Wow, that hasn't happened since..." Jo paused as she glanced toward the hill. "Um, for a while."

"Who's Gertrude?"

"It's the name she gave her Jet Ski."

"She named it Gertrude? That's awesome. My best friend's cat is named Gertrude." Allie was having a hard time locking her thoughts of Kate away in that part of her brain marked *don't go there*, so she surrendered and went there. "What's her story?"

"Kate? Not much to tell." Jo shrugged. "She's a great boss, keeps to herself mostly, and adores Gizmo."

That response was protectively general, and it didn't supply the information she was fishing for, so she took the lead. "Too bad about Brooke, huh?" There, she'd cast the lure. Now she waited to see if Jo would take the bait.

"Did you know her?"

"No, not really."

Jo remained quiet for a few beats. "She was the nicest person I have ever met. She's the reason I'm here. Actually, why most of us are here. She volunteered for a program that helped Los Angeles homeless LGBTQ+ youth get back on their feet. I was fifteen, she was my counselor, and my first thought was that she smelled nice. My second was that she was kind, and up until that point in my life, I hadn't known much kindness. We were all devastated when she died. It about destroyed Kate. But we all know she's still here watching over us in her own way."

Wow, what an endorsement. Allie reflected back to all six of her exes. She could honestly say that at the time of the relationship, she'd loved each of them but had never felt crippled when the love affair ended. Bruised ego, hurt, and angry, yes, but if any of them passed away, would it destroy her? No, was the honest answer, and she didn't know what that really said about her past relationships. Maybe that was a reflection of her and not them, or maybe it was a reflection on just not finding the right "one" yet. She hoped it was the latter of the two.

"So." Jo turned to Allie as they reached her casita. "I was wondering if after dinner tonight, you would like to come to my cottage and have a drink, and maybe we could go for another late-night walk on the beach?"

"Jo." Allie gazed at her. She could tell from their interactions that Jo was a good person. A gentle soul and someone who seemed to care. But she also sensed Jo was a player, and although it had been years since she'd felt the beautiful sensation of another woman's touch, she didn't want a hookup. "You seem amazing, and you're sexy as hell, but I just don't—"

"You can stop right there." Jo held up her hand. "I know where this is going, and I don't need to hear the rest of the sentence."

"It's just not where I'm at right now or why I came here. But I'll still take you up on that after-dinner walk on the beach if you're still okay with that?"

Jo averted her eyes. "Yeah, sure, I think that would be nice."

"I think so too." Allie placed a finger under Jo's chin and lifted her head. "See you then, okay?"

Jo nodded. "Yeah, see you then," she said in a soft voice before turning and hurrying away.

Allie sighed with both relief and concern. She didn't mean to hurt Jo's feelings, but the longer she kept that flame stoked, the messier things would get between them. And she genuinely liked Jo. If the after-dinner walk between them this evening didn't end up being too awkward, maybe they could settle into a nice friendship.

She entered her casita, flung the backpack on the table, grabbed her phone, and flopped on the couch to entertain her latest unhealthy obsession. She googled Suzanne Bennett again, and this time bypassed the distracting photos and searched for more details about her life. A task that she soon learned was a bit impossible to achieve. None of the articles she clicked on gave her a sense of who Kate really was, beyond her wild side and brief brushes with the law in the form of a couple DUIs. But she did find abundant articles that took a deep dive into her father's life, and through those, Allie pieced together a pretty good picture of what Kate's upbringing must have been like.

She tossed the phone on the coffee table and leaned her head back against the cushions as insecurities of never being good enough for someone like Kate surfaced. Even if she did resolve Kate's misconception of her, an heiress to a billion-dollar company would never be interested in someone like her beyond a hookup or two. And even if they did miraculously last beyond that, she could only imagine what Kate's father would think of her at family functions. Someone like Allie just didn't have the right pedigree to be with a Bennett. She closed her eyes as Kate's sparkling blues danced in her head and triggered a slight spasm much lower. Too bad she'd probably never know what it was like to ease that ache with the person causing it.

❖

"B7," the perky blonde behind the bingo wheel called out.

"Bingo," Linda announced as her arms shot up in triumph.

Jo approached the table dangling a Rainbow's End key chain on her finger and handed it to Linda with a wink.

"Well, well." Allie nudged Linda. "Looks like Jo might be interested in you."

"I know, that was weird. What happened? Did you two have a falling out or something?" Linda tossed the key chain to Sheri, who was holding her hand out gesturing to see it.

"What? No, there was never an *us* to fall out of. In fact." She raised a brow. "I think you two would make the perfect couple. Jo's really nice."

"What aren't you telling me?"

"Nothing, I swear. Jo just doesn't…she um, it's just that…" Allie sighed. "That's not why I'm here."

"Hmm, all-women resort, beautiful butch in hot pursuit, single status marked on your social media page, and that's not why you're here? I'd say I get it, but I really don't."

"Linda, let her be," Jan scolded. "Not everyone has raging hormones like you do."

"It's true." Linda chuckled. "I can't help it."

"Well, I say go for it. Like you said: lesbian resort, beautiful butch, single in status." Allie bounced the sentiment right back at her.

"You're right. Ladies." Linda pushed back from the table, stood, and glanced in Jo's direction. "I'll be right back."

"Yeah, right. We won't wait up for you," Jan called as Linda scurried away. "I swear, that girl could give Aphrodite a run for her money."

"Well, it does seem like she's got the magic touch." Allie watched Linda whisper something in Jo's ear. A beat later, Jo placed her arm around Linda's waist and escorted her away. "I definitely wouldn't wait up for her," Allie said to the group as an unexpected twinge flashed through her of…what? Jealousy? No, she concluded. She had no feelings for Jo, and if she and Linda hit it off, she would be happy for them. If anything, the emotion gripping her seemed to reflect the emptiness that had been pulling on her. Maybe envy was the more appropriate word.

"Okay, if anyone wants new cards for this next game," the same blonde announced as she began spinning the bingo wheel. "Come up and grab them. The winner of this round will get a Rainbow's End teddy bear." She held up a small, fluffy, light brown bear with a bandana around its neck with the resort's logo embroidered on the fabric.

"Oh my God, I'm in love with that bear. If any of you win, I'll trade you something for it," Jan said.

"Actually." Allie stood and arched her back. "I think I'll go for a walk on the beach."

"Was it something we said?" Jan said in a soft voice.

"No." Allie reassured them with a shake of her head. "Not at all. I just want to sleep in a bit before going diving tomorrow, and a walk on the beach before bed sounds wonderfully relaxing. Besides, with me out, you have better odds of winning the bear." She grabbed her phone and slid it into the back pocket of her shorts.

"Your sacrifice on my behalf is duly noted," Jan said. "Have a nice night, Allie, we'll see you tomorrow."

"Sounds good. Good night, ladies." Allie excused herself and headed to the beach. As she walked toward the dock, she decided to turn right instead of left and meander down the section of the island where Kate lived.

She kicked off her sandals, hooked them between her fingers, and enjoyed the sensation of her bare feet sinking in the fine textured sand. She glanced out into the darkness of the ocean as she strolled to the end of the beach and flopped down a few yards from the walkway that led to Kate's sprawling house.

She sat in the shadows of the moonlight, folded her knees into her chest, inhaled a deep breath, and thought about the restaurant. It was a place and a career that her parents had chosen, and even though she was born into it, did she really want to walk in their shoes the rest of her life? No, was the answer that whispered back to her every time she asked the question. Now that her dad was gone, she would finish the obligation she held for her mom, then sell the place when her mother passed and finally have a life of her own. A life that would make her happy in ways she had yet to know. Hell, maybe by then, she'd run away to Nassau and see if Olivia's dive shop needed an extra instructor. Unlike most people she knew in LA, she didn't seek fame and fortune. She just wanted to do something that made her soul content and live in a place that spoke to her. The diner and her studio apartment in east LA did neither.

Chapter Eight

The resort at night was stunningly beautiful. Years ago, Kate had flown in a lighting designer from Hollywood to work with her landscaper and create a masterpiece of eye-catching artistry that gave the property the right mix of romantic flare. She and Brooke used to stroll the beach every evening, then saunter through the resort, admiring the way the well-placed colorful lights and gas tiki torches transformed the place into a magical paradise. She had stopped the nightly routine after Brooke passed because it was too painful but picked it up again when Gizmo's vet told her exercise would do Giz some good during her recovery.

"Come on, Gizzy, time for our walk."

Gizmo took the lead as they jogged down the walkway from her patio until the sand slowed their stride, and the lapping of the ocean around Kate's bare feet caused her to pause. The water was warm and soothing, and the sound of the crashing waves was peaceful. She focused into the darkness, but instead of conjuring up her nightly image of Brooke, her mind filled with visions of Allie. If not for the fact that she'd lied about treasure hunting—and seemed interested in Jo—Kate probably would have pursued getting to know her better while she was here. Of all the people to wake her desires. There had to be a cruel joke in there somewhere, she grumbled to herself as they headed toward the pier. No, her best play with Allie was to stay as far away from her as possible. She would be gone in a few days, and all the emotions that she'd stirred up would settle back down, and her life would return to what had become her normal routine.

When they reached the pier, Gizmo lifted her head, sniffed, then took off running down the dock, grunting and squealing loudly. "Gizmo," Kate scolded in a loud whisper as she chased her. "Gizmo? What are you doing? Get back here!"

When they were parallel with Allie's boat, a shadowy figure jumped out, startling Kate. "Holy shit, Carla. What are you doing here?" Kate slapped her hand to her chest as she tried to calm her racing heart.

"Oh my God, could you both be any louder?" Carla grabbed Kate's forearm and spun her back in the direction of the beach with Gizmo in tow. "And what do you mean, what am I doing out here? I'm sabotaging a guest's boat. On your orders, might I add. That's what I'm doing out here," she whispered as Gizmo continued to grunt and squeal by her side.

"Shh." Kate bent with fingers to their lips in an attempt to silence her. "Gizmo, enough." She rewarded Giz with a pat to her head when she stopped oinking, then turned her attention to Carla. "I thought you were going to do that later tonight, when everyone's sleeping?"

"It's ten o'clock, and for me, that's late enough. I'm getting up early tomorrow to join the sunrise yoga class." Carla pinched her side. "I need to get rid of this love handle that seems to have permanently affixed itself to my body. Although, the last time I took one of Anna's yoga classes, I was so sore, I waddled like a fucking penguin for two days."

"I don't remember that."

"Yeah, well, maybe that's a good thing," she said with a tilt of her head as they began walking up the beach toward Kate's house.

"So?"

Carla paused and glanced at Kate. "So what? You'll have to give me more of a hint than that if you want me to participate in a guessing game."

"Did you…you know, *fix* the boat?" Kate leaned in and whispered.

Carla displayed a screwdriver that had been discreetly tucked in the back of her wraparound skirt. "You'd be amazed what you can do with a simple little hardware device. It's not hi-tech sabotage, but it's effective."

"What'd ya do?"

"Disconnected the boat's battery cable, which she'll never figure out because the battery's in an area that wasn't easy to get to. If *I* had trouble locating it, she'll never find it. Plus, it's a simple fix for when she needs to use the boat to get back to Nassau."

"You're a genius, Carla. Thanks for doing that."

"Uh-huh, and I'll expect a sabotage pay bump in my next check."

Kate cocked her head. "Actually, how would you feel if I gave you Gretta?"

Carla placed her hand on her chest as she caught her breath. "What, are you kidding?"

"No, I'm not. That Jet Ski's been sitting there waiting for someone to give it the love and attention Brooke did. It's…" Kate averted her eyes as she glanced in the direction of the Jet Ski dock. "What she would want and it's time."

"First of all, thank you. You know I'll take good care of Gretta. And second, you doing okay, boss?"

"Yeah, I just…I just think it's time." But was there really such a thing as ever enough time when it came to healing from losing the love of her life? No, of course not. Time might soften the sting, it might even distract the mind and refocus its attention elsewhere, but healing the heart seemed beyond its abilities. Because no matter how much time passed, a certain song, a distinct smell or a lingering thought would always whisk Kate back to a moment in time that she'd shared with Brooke. Hell, everywhere she went on the cay was like walking in her footsteps. Healing a broken heart, she concluded, was an illusion. Once cracked, even if glued back together, was never the same.

Carla draped an arm around Kate's shoulders as they continued to stroll down the beach. "Well, thank you. Maybe I'll take her out for a spin tomorrow."

"You know where the key is. Take it and keep it. She's all yours."

"Anyone ever tell you you're the best boss in the world?"

"No, and for the record, I never aspired to be a boss. Most of my life, I could barely manage myself, much less other people." When Carla had insisted on calling her boss instead of Kate, it had bothered her. The term had once reminded her too much of her father and the physical and emotional absence that came with that label. Her entire childhood, she'd been repeatedly told—as though the explanation in some way justified the action—that he was busy being the boss of the family's business empire, and therefore could not be around for the important milestones in her life. It took Kate a while for the label to shift from a feeling of resentment to one of endearment.

"Well, congratulations on your graduation to the real world, boss." Carla leaned in and kissed her on the cheek. "Because you really are the best. Now then, all this espionage stuff has worn me out, so I'm going to head on back. This girl's gotta get her beauty sleep." She turned and began jogging toward the resort.

"Thanks again, Carla."

"What's the plan with Casita Four now that she's grounded?" Carla spun around and walked backward.

"Nothing, she'll enjoy her stay like the other guests, and the day before she leaves, I'll make sure her boat magically gets fixed."

"Uh-huh, you mean *I'll* make sure her boat gets fixed."

"Yes, of course, you'll make sure."

"Hmm, you know what? Your yacht's looking like good hush money."

Kate threw her head back and laughed. "Yeah, that'll never happen."

Carla shrugged. "A girl can dream." She turned back around and continued heading up the sand toward the resort.

Gizmo took a few steps in her direction, then turned and settled next to Kate. She bent and scratched Giz's head. "I know she's your buddy, but next time, you need to listen to me when I call your name." She moved her fingers under Gizzy's chin. She knew Gizmo had a mind of her own and was about as trainable as a rock. But that was one of the things Kate loved about her. She had a free spirit that reminded her of Brooke. "Yeah, you're not spoiled at all, are you?" Gizmo grunted. Kate chuckled. "Come on, you, let's go home."

As they retraced their steps, Gizmo once again began sniffing the air, then scurried into the shadows beyond the walkway that led to her patio.

"Gizmo! Gizmo. What has gotten into you tonight?" Kate said as she followed into the darkness and startled as she saw the moonlit silhouette of a person sitting on the beach.

"Well, hello, Gizmo."

The soft recognizable voice made Kate's stomach instantly churn from equal parts excitement and dread. Shit, it was Allie. Kate was not in the mood to see her again. She had spent all afternoon anguishing over whether she should apologize for her abrupt exit or continue to self-righteously wallow in her anger. In her former life, she would have handled the conflicting feelings by numbing out until the issue became a nonissue. Nowadays, she was forced to deal with the uncomfortableness of her emotions and actions. Adulting was so overrated at times.

She hunched her shoulders and decided on the one action item that seemed to be the best compromise: she'd be professionally polite and nothing more. After all, the hunter was now grounded, and even if sabotaging her boat was a power play and not the most mature way to handle the situation, it had eased Kate's anxiety.

"Hello, Allie," Kate kept her voice soft but flat as she approached. "What are you doing out here? Were you not enjoying bingo night?"

"I was, it's just…the ocean was calling to me more than the game was. And since walking on an uncrowded pristine beach is a pleasure I really have in LA, I thought I'd take advantage of it while I'm here. Plus, I'm not going diving until later tomorrow morning, and the thought of sleeping in is very appealing. I thought a walk before bed would be relaxing and help knock me out for the night."

"I can attest that late-night beach strolls work wonders. Well." She tapped her thigh, hoping Gizmo would take the hint and come to her side so she could leave before any more exchange happened between them. "It was nice seeing you again. Have a good evening."

"Thanks, you too. And it's nice to officially meet the pig I've heard so much about."

"Yes, Gizmo is rather spectacular, isn't she?" Kate said. "Well, come on, Gizzy, let's get on back to the house and leave the guests alone." She again slapped her thigh, this time a little louder, and turned away. "Have a nice night, Allie."

"Jo told me the story of her washing up onshore one day, is that true?"

She fought the urge to continue walking and pretend she hadn't heard the question. It was a move right out of her former life's playbook and had more than once gotten her out of a situation she didn't want to deal with.

She pinched the bridge of her nose and heard Carla's scolding voice in her head telling her to grow up and act her age, to which Kate had once replied, "My physical or my mental age?" She let out a defeated breath, turned around, and decided on maturity. "It is. Pig Beach isn't too far from here, so our best guess is the current pulled her out to sea, and she somehow made it to our shore."

"Well," Allie cooed in a higher singsong pitch as she scratched under Gizmo's chin. "She's a lucky girl."

Having Allie gush on Gizmo was endearing to watch. Kate had learned at an early age that one of the best ways to read a person was to watch how they interacted with animals. If any of her nannies took issues with Simon, her rather unruly childhood tabby cat, she'd made sure their time of employment was short-lived. "Well, again, have a good evening. Gizmo, come. Gizmo," she said in a loud stern voice, hoping Giz would understand she was starting to skate on thin ice. Gizmo grunted and slowly trotted over to her. "Good girl." She showered her with praise as they walked away from Allie and the uncomfortable sexual feelings that once again began to stir.

"Come on, I'll race you to the top of…" Kate tilted her head as she focused on Gizmo's mouth. Or more to the point, the unidentifiable object sticking out of her mouth. "What do you got there, girl?" She reached down, but Gizzy turned her head and began trotting away. "Gizmo, come here. Gizmo." She ran in a circle, chasing Giz in a game that the pig probably thought was a fun form of keep-away, until Gizmo finally surrendered and let Kate retrieve the item from her mouth. "You've got to be shitting me," she said as she held a slobbery cell phone in her hands. "Gizzy, stop taking things, or I'm going to have to start locking you up." Kate sternly scolded her with empty threats. Again, she could just continue walking and pretend Gizmo hadn't stolen Allie's phone and have it magically appear the next morning as though she'd found it in the sand. But Kate knew how frantic she would be if she thought, even for a minute, that she had lost her phone.

"Come on," she said in defeat to Gizmo as they headed back to Allie. "You need to apologize for your behavior, and I need to stop letting you get away with so much mischief. We both need therapy."

"Looking for this?" Kate displayed the phone when she noticed Allie searching the sand.

Allie glanced up. "My phone. How did you—"

"Gizmo. She likes to take things that don't belong to her." Kate handed the phone back. "I rubbed it on my shorts to get off her slobber, but you might want to wash it off a bit more when you get back to your casita. And if there's any damage, I'll make sure you are fully compensated. Gizmo apologizes for her kleptomaniac tendencies. It's something we're working on." Kate stiffened a bit and braced for an unpleasant response from Allie, and truthfully, she wouldn't blame her.

"No worries at all." Allie chuckled. "I'm just relieved to have it back. I thought I lost it in the sand, and my whole life is in this phone."

Phew. Kate softened her stance. "Nope, not lost, just stolen from a thief in the shape of a pig. Now, say you're sorry, Gizmo, so we can go home." Gizmo grunted. "My apologizes again. Have a good rest of your evening." Kate turned to walk away when Allie spoke up.

"Kate, I have something to show you, and it'll only take a minute of your time."

She turned as Allie extended a hand, shoving her phone in Kate's face. "What am I supposed to be looking at?" She leaned back, trying to focus on the screen.

Allie pushed the phone a little closer. "Look in the lower right corner."

Kate gazed at a picture of a metal detector under the words, *free with minimum 5-day gear rental.* "What does that have to do with anything?" A quiver of annoyance shot through her. Why in the world would Allie show her an ad for a metal detector when she knew her feelings about treasure hunting?

"It's from the dive shop where I rented my gear." Allie turned her phone around, ran her finger over her screen, then displayed another page. "And this is my list of the items I actually ordered, and as you can see, a metal detector is not one of them."

"I don't understand what..." Kate glanced at the screen as realization of what Allie was saying sunk in. "Oh." Shit.

"I'm trying to show you what I was trying to tell you on the boat earlier today when you wouldn't let me get a word in edgewise. The metal detector was included in my scuba package. It's their special free item of the month if you rent the gear for five days or more. It may be sitting on my boat, but I swear to you that I haven't used it. You have my word on that. I am not, nor have I ever been, a treasure hunter. Please believe me when I say your assumption of me is a misunderstanding."

"I, um," Kate mumbled. Did she feel a little embarrassed? Why, yes. Yes, she did. Was she going to admit it? No, of course not. Besides, people lied all the time to cover up their true intentions. Even if the metal detector did come with the package deal, it didn't mean Allie had to take it? Right?

They stood in silence, the agitated storm that had been brewing in Kate eased a bit with the explanation, but having the device sitting on Allie's boat was still troubling. At any moment, the temptation for Allie to try it out was within arm's reach. The lure of the unknown was too enticing. No, she reasoned as she countered her rising guilt, sabotaging the boat was the right thing to do. An insurance policy for a messy situation that was shut down before it ever happened. *Oh, and note to self: new resort policy, no more private guest boats allowed on the island.* "Well, thank you for clarifying that." It might not have been the apology that Allie wanted, but for right now, it was all she had to give.

"I wanted you to know that I was telling you the truth. It was important to me." Allie pocketed her phone, let a comfortable pause settle between them, and seemed to put the subject to rest as she tilted her head toward the sky. "You know, I can't tell you how many times in my life I've stared at the night sky, and I've never seen so many stars and such beauty as here."

Relieved at the subject change, Kate glanced upward. She was familiar with the beauty of the night sky because she and Brooke would sit out on the porch and routinely stargaze. Brooke used to tell her the vastness of the sky was a good reminder of how insignificant she was in the universe and how... "It keeps you humble," she said.

Allie glanced over. "What?"

"The stars. The vastness. It keeps you humble. Are you a stargazer?"

"No, not in the real sense. But when I was a kid, I wanted a telescope really bad. I was into this TV show where one of the lead characters was an astronomer. I thought, yeah, that's going to be me when I grow up." Allie turned to face her. "But I never got a telescope, and my life took a very different turn."

"I'm sorry to hear that." Kate remembered the huge telescope in her father's study that sat untouched and represented nothing more to him than a coat hanger. Yet, every time she expressed interest in it, she was shooed away and told that it wasn't a toy to be played with. After she and Brooke had settled on the cay and she'd realized how much Brooke enjoyed stargazing, she'd offered to buy her a telescope as grandiose as her father's. Brooke had declined all her offers and told her she was missing the point: "I don't want a fancy telescope, babe. Stargazing is about snuggling together under their blanket of beauty. All I need is you, my phone, and a star app."

Allie shrugged. "I haven't thought about that for years. But being out here, where the stars are so amazing, it kinda brings it up again. LA skies have too much light pollution and haze."

"Yes, the skies around here are breathtaking."

"I once read somewhere that many of the smaller prohibition rumrunner operations would use the stars to help them navigate through the Bahama waters."

"I've never heard that one, but…" Kate cleared her throat as she directed the conversation down another road. One laced with curiosity. This time last night, Jo had been giving Allie a tour of the island, and yet tonight, here she stood. Alone and in the shadows. "If you ever want to know more about the Bahamas, Jo's a good one to hit up. She's a bit of a history buff, so she could tell you all the colorful stories of the pirates, rumrunners, and the age of lawlessness of the Bahamas."

"She shared a bit of that last night when she gave me a tour around the cay. In fact, she was going to give me another this evening after dinner, but let's just say she got distracted with someone else."

Kate understood the unspoken words in that statement, and the feeling of relief did not go unnoticed. So far, the evening had been full of interesting surprises. "Ah, hence you being out here all by yourself. Well, I could share with you all the things I know about the area, but it might not be as entertaining as Jo's version."

"I can google the history of the Bahamas, how about you tell me the history of your cay, what brought you here, and why you built the resort?"

Kate tensed. It wasn't like anyone doing a search on her couldn't connect the dots that she was Suzanne Bennett, and this had been her parents' island at one time. And the paparazzi pictures and gossip articles about her were out there for those who wanted to take a deep dive into her life. Hell, even not so deep. Still, she decided to keep the conversation about her life on the surface. She shrugged. "The resort was built about twelve years ago. All the staff has, for the most part, been here since the beginning. Mila and Kim, our full-time physician we call Doc, were the first to join, and since everyone lives on the island, they like to think of themselves as the family they weren't born into. They're a tight-knit group."

"I can tell. So what made you want to build it?"

She could have been honest with Allie and told her about running away from a life that she'd lost control of. About being hounded by the paparazzi and press until the lines between what they wrote about her and who she thought she was had become blurred. She could have told her about Brooke and about the second chance this cay had given her on life. About how she knew she had been born to privilege and how she'd watched that same privilege destroy the foundation of her family. And although she was grateful that the money afforded her the luxury of never having to worry about finances, she was also well aware that money alone didn't solve everything. It couldn't give her the childhood she'd so desperately longed for, and in the end, it couldn't save Brooke.

She turned to face Allie and stared into the eyes of someone who seemed genuinely interested, but instead of letting her in, she waved a dismissive hand and sidestepped the question. "I think it was one of those *why not* build it situations. It's a great location, and it allows women to feel comfortable amongst their own."

"Well, as a guest, I can honestly say that I've felt comfortable from the moment I stepped onto the cay."

"Then I have done my job successfully." She smiled as she averted her eyes. Being on the beach, stargazing, Allie's questions, emerging feelings…they were all making her a little dizzy as old memories began clashing with new ones. "Well, anyway, I should be heading back. So for the last time, I hope you enjoy the rest of your evening, Allie." She let her eyes linger on her longer than she intended, but she couldn't help it. It was like trying to pull her attention away from the magnificence of a blooming rose.

"I will, you too."

Kate nodded, and as she headed up the path to her house, Brooke popped up next to her. "She seems nice, and she's making you nervous. Why?" Brooke said as she flanked her.

"She's not making me nervous." Kate huffed defensively as she glanced over.

Brooke took a moment to extend her arms and twirl like she always had at the end of their walk. "Oh, she's totally making you nervous. You like her, don't you?"

"Stop." Kate waved at the voice in her head.

"Babe," Brooke said as they approached the house and headed for the patio. "There's nothing wrong with that."

Kate froze and turned. "There's everything wrong with that. Don't you see? I can't have feelings for anyone else. I'm still in love with you."

Brooke approached. "And I still love you. But she can give you something I can't."

"No one can give me what I want except you."

"Babe…"

Kate turned in denial as she and Gizmo flopped into their lounge chairs. She folded her arms over her chest and stared into the darkness.

"Babe," Brooke repeated as she sat next to Gizmo.

"No, Brooke. I won't do this to you."

"But don't you see. You're not doing it to me, you're doing it to yourself."

Kate closed her eyes as tears dripped down her cheeks. For the past five years, she had created a life that had teetered with one foot in the past and one in the present. Was it halfway delusional? Sure, but she didn't care. And up until Allie had arrived, nothing had challenged her. Well, Carla had called her out a time or two, but still.

When she opened her eyes and turned with another rebuttal forming on her lips, Brooke was gone, but Gizmo's ears perked up as she grunted at her. Kate pressed her head farther into the cushion of the chair and exhaled a deep breath. "What am I going to do, Giz? Any words of advice?" She flopped her head toward Gizmo, who grunted once more, rubbed her face on the chair's fabric, and farted.

Chapter Nine

Allie stepped out of her casita, squinted at the rising sun, and pushed the oversized plastic sunglasses farther up her nose. She had hoped to sleep in this morning, but after she got up to pee, she couldn't settle her mind, so she'd surrendered and decided to start her day earlier than she planned. She paused for a moment and took a deep breath to appreciate the smell of the clean salty air and the sound of the crashing waves instead of the car horns that greeted her every morning in LA. There wasn't a cloud in the sky, the wind was almost nonexistent, and the warmth of the sun felt good on her skin. She couldn't have asked for a more perfect day.

"Ah, to be rich and have the option of where to live, huh, Dad?" she mused as she craned her neck toward the backpack slung over one shoulder. She gave the bulge from his urn a loving pat. "Come on. Let's get you to where you want to be."

As she meandered down the path past the kitchen, she saw Mila out front, bowl in one hand and scissors in another, bent over and cutting some herbs from a raised garden bed. She approached. "Hi, Mila, I met you the other night, and I just wanted to tell you again how much I enjoy your cooking."

Mila raised her head just enough to flick a glance at Allie, then returned to her task, clearly uninterested in what she had to say.

Although a feeling of awkwardness settled in, Allie was not deterred. "Anyway, I think you're an amazing chef and I just wanted you to know that. Sorry to bother you."

Mila let out a sigh, placed her scissors in the bowl, and straightened. She cocked a knee, and her face hardened in an expression Allie interpreted as more than just mild irritability, as though she had been interrupted from her morning meditation.

Oh-kay...so much for that. After an uncomfortable several seconds, Allie began backing away until she noticed Mila's eyes widen and become fixed on her necklace. Allie cupped the shell pendant. "It was my father's. It's a—"

"Sea turtle." Mila said, then gazed at Allie. The expression that moments ago held a sternness that could rival a nun on a rampage had softened.

"Yes, he believed we are descendants of a small tribe of islanders. This pendant is a tribute to a handful who lost their lives in a last stand to save their people. My dad used to tell me the turtles carried their souls to their final destination."

Mila nodded, and Allie could have sworn she saw sadness in her eyes. "They carry little souls too." The words were barely audible. A beat later, she blinked, picked up her scissors and waved a hand, shooing Allie away. "Now go on, get. You're standing in my sun. Got's no time to talk to anyone, I'm busy," she said as she bent back down and started snipping more herbs.

As Allie continued backing away, she noticed a small tattoo on the underside of Mila's right wrist. It was faded and hard to make out against the contrast of her dark and wrinkled skin, but Allie was sure it was an outline of a sea turtle with the name "Jacob" under the design.

There's a sad story there, Allie mused as she headed toward the dock. *One that would probably shine a light on why Mila was so cantankerous. But she would bet her life's savings it was a story no one at the resort knew, and one Mila would take with her to her grave.*

As she passed the dining area and nodded to two of the staff tearing down the table from last night's bingo game, her mind wandered to Linda and Jo and wondered if they had hooked up for the evening. And as if on cue, Linda came strolling around the corner from the direction of the crew's cottages.

"Hey, Allie." Linda waved enthusiastically. "Off for a morning dive?"

"I am. And dare I ask, how did things go with Jo?"

Linda smiled. "God, that woman knows my body better than I do. She introduced me to hidden spots I never knew I had." Linda playfully fanned her face.

"Wow, I'd say things are going pretty good, then." Allie chuckled at Linda's not-so-subtle glow.

"We're getting together this afternoon. She's going to give me a private paddleboard lesson."

"Sounds..." Allie paused as her imagination wandered down a few interesting roads. "Like a wonderful time. Will I see you later this evening for dinner?" She took a few steps in the direction of the dock.

"Yep. Unless of course, Jo and I hook up for a little rendezvous, if you know what I mean." Linda winked.

"I'm pretty sure I do," Allie said lightheartedly as she waved good-bye. She was happy for the two of them. They seemed made for each other. Unlike her and Kate, she thought as she glanced at the yacht. The woman was a bit of an enigma, that was for sure. One minute, she felt heat from Kate, and just as fast, a cold breeze could blow between them. But there was something about last night that seemed to thaw Kate's icy edge.

Allie jumped aboard her boat, placed the backpack on the deck by the helm, unzipped the bag, and double-checked the urn. "Okay, Dad, here we go." She exhaled and tried to shake an unexpected bit of sadness. It was time to completely say her good-byes.

"Hmm?" she said as she tried to turn over the ignition. "Shit." She looked around at nothing in particular, then made a second attempt. "No…no, no, no!" She tried another five times, pausing intermittingly. "*Damn it.*" She slapped at the dash because why not? Sometimes, the action started the computer at the restaurant when it froze. "Fuck." She grunted when nothing happened. She punched at the dash one last time, grabbed her phone, and called Olivia.

"Olivia here."

"Hey, Olivia, it's Allie." She tried to calm the boiling frustration that was teetering on the verge of bitchiness. "You rented me your boat a couple of days ago and I—"

"Oh hey, Allie," Olivia interrupted. "How's she holding up?"

A few choice words to describe her true feelings about the boat formed on the tip of her tongue, but she forced a smile and tried to tamp down her growing agitation. "Well, that's just it. The boat was doing fine, but today, it won't start."

"What do you mean it won't start? I checked her over from bow to stern before I handed her off to you."

"I'm sure you did." Oops, that came out a bit too snappy. *Take a breath. Smile.* "But right now, it won't start. At all. Any suggestions on what to do?"

"Try turning it over again and let me hear if she makes any particular noise."

"Okay." Allie did as she was told.

"I didn't hear anything."

"I know, that's what I'm trying to tell you. Nothing happens when I try to start the boat."

"Shit. Um, well, I'm in Miami right now working a private charter for the next three days. Is there anyone at the resort who knows their way around a boat who can look her over?"

"I don't know." Maybe she could flag Jo down this morning and have her take a look at it.

Olivia let out a heavy sigh. "Okay, I tell you what, as soon as I get back to Nassau, I'll take one of the shop's dive boats and come over and have a look. I'm really sorry about this, Allie, and of course, I'll refund your money."

She felt bad that Olivia would do that because she seemed like a genuinely nice person, but then again, the boat wasn't working the one time she needed it the most, and besides, that refund could go back to her mom. "Thanks, Olivia. I appreciate that."

"Yeah, I mean, it's the least I can do. I feel bad about this."

"Well, she got me here, so she picked the right place to break down." If Olivia managed to get the boat up and running in three days, she would still have time to bury her dad and fulfill his wish before her time on the island was up.

"Hey, I gotta go. I'll text you in a few days when I'm on my way. And again, I'm so sorry about that."

"It's okay." Allie reassured her, even though it wasn't, but what else was she going to say? She needed the boat fixed, and Olivia seemed like her only answer. Allie disconnected the call and glanced out into the ocean. She contemplated whether she could just scuba to the coordinates from the cay but realized just as quickly that she would probably run out of air before she made it back. That meant she would have to snorkel the remaining distance, and that made her a bit uncomfortable. Not that she feared sharks; she didn't. She'd had several peaceful encounters while scuba diving. But being submerged in open water, as opposed to being on the surface, was always the safer option. No, she was grounded for a few days until Olivia fixed the boat.

Allie kicked the dash for good measure, tried one last time to turn over the ignition, then surrendered. She slumped against the side of the boat, tightly folded her arms, and pouted. She should have known better than to trust Shelly with something as important as lining up her boat and gear. Reba was right: exes need to stay in the rearview mirror. She let out another breath of agitated angst and scrubbed her fingers through her hair when she noticed a sea ray close to the surface, leisurely swimming by. Maybe the morning didn't have to be a total loss. She could do a shore dive and enjoy the aquatic life in the lagoon. It would calm her down, and Jo did say there was an abundance of sea creatures that called this area home.

Maybe she would even crash Jo and Linda's paddleboard lesson this afternoon and gain a few pointers on a sport she had always wanted to try. After all, it wasn't like the delay would affect her dad in any way. She glanced at her backpack. "Sorry, Dad, change of plans," she said as she headed to her tanks but paused as she heard the sound of wood creaking. She craned her neck and saw Kate driving her golf cart down the dock. Her one arm rested on a cooler that sat beside her.

When Kate glanced her way, her eyes widened. "Allie? Hi, I, uh, I thought you said you weren't going diving until a little later?" Kate parked the cart parallel to her yacht.

"I was, but I woke up earlier than anticipated and thought I'd get a jump on the day. But my plans have been a bit derailed. My boat won't start."

"Oh, really? It won't start?" Kate said, and Allie could have sworn her lips turned up ever so slightly. "Well, that's not good."

"No, it's not. And the woman I rented it from won't be able to come take a look at it for a few days."

"I'm sorry to hear that." Kate hoisted the cooler out of the golf cart and hopped aboard her yacht.

"Do you know anything about boats?"

"What, beyond operating one?" Kate called over her shoulder as she busied herself in the cabin.

"Yeah, like, mechanically."

Kate stepped off the yacht and began untying the dock line from the cleat that secured the boat's bow. "Sorry, I just know how to enjoy them, not fix them."

"Yeah, me too." Allie sighed. "Oh well, guess I'll spend the morning diving in the lagoon. I already saw a ray swim by a moment ago."

"You'd be amazed at how much sea life calls this little cove home."

"Yeah, so I've heard."

Kate strolled to the stern of the yacht and reached for the remaining line. "Well, have a nice day," she said in what Allie perceived as a semi-dismissive tone.

"Here." Allie hopped off her boat. "Let me help you." She hustled over.

"I got it." Kate shooed as she stepped around her.

Their hands entwined, and the jolt that was now becoming familiar every time she and Kate touched sent a shiver up her body. Time froze, and the only thing Allie became aware of at that moment was the slightest hint of patchouli in the air and the softness of Kate's skin. God, Kate gave her the feels.

"I, um," Kate said as she slowly pulled her hand away. "I could have gotten that."

"I know, but it's always easier with an extra pair of hands. Now go on, get aboard, and I'll toss the line to you."

Kate paused, glanced at her, and nodded. "Yeah. Okay, thanks."

She jumped aboard as Allie bent down and reversed the figure eight loops that wove around the cleat when a motion caught her eye. She tilted her head enough to catch Kate talking to herself in a rather animated way. Allie chuckled and thought of the time she was in the diner's kitchen, cooking a batch of pasta. It was the morning after she and Shelly had a huge fight, and she was reenacting all of the snarky exchanges between them when her mom walked in, froze, made the symbol of a cross over her chest, and muttered something about Allie's father's genes playing out as she'd scurried away.

"Ready?" Allie stood and gestured to the rope in hand.

"Actually," Kate said. "Have you ever been wreck diving?"

"No."

"There's a plane less than an hour from here that I like to go free diving at. You could bring a tank and join me. Or if you want, I can teach you how to free dive. It's only about a twenty-foot depth, so it's totally doable for a beginner."

"Free dive? Seriously?"

"Sure, it's easy, and it's just like scuba diving, except of course, you have to hold your breath."

"Oh, right, that little detail." Allie took a moment to think about the offer. It would be nice spending more time with Kate, but she really didn't want to be out with her on the ocean again if she turned all ice queen and accusatory. Still, her gut told there was a connection between them that was worth exploring. "Yeah, I, um, sure, why not. I'd love to. Let me grab my mask and fins." She resecured the line, hurried to her boat, snagged her gear from the container, and shrugged on her backpack. "Another change of plans, Dad. I'm taking you on a yacht ride." Allie knew if her dad was still alive, he'd probably love being on a boat that signified a status he was never able to achieve. She returned to the rope, untied it, and with one big hop, landed on the platform at the stern of the yacht. "Where do you store your dock lines?"

"Coil it and hang it on the hook on the deck. You can't miss it." Kate called from over her shoulder as she headed to the helm. "Let me get her away from the dock, then I'll show you around, and we can have some breakfast. Have you eaten yet?"

"No, I haven't." Allie secured the rope and took a moment to glance around at her surroundings. She used to envy those who docked their luxury boats in Long Beach not far from Shelly's dive shop and wondered what it would be like to own one. If she did, she would live on it and spend her days relaxing on the water and scuba diving as much as possible. Why own a vessel that cost more than most houses if it couldn't be enjoyed and appreciated on a full-time basis? She was taken aback when Shelly had informed her that most of the boats at the harbor sat moored and empty throughout the year, if not longer. Seemed as though wealth was wasted on those who never seemed to appreciate what they had.

When she entered the cabin, she did a slow three-sixty and marveled at the luxurious amenities. As if she needed a reminder, the difference between their economic backgrounds was made abundantly clear, and an awkwardness washed over her as that twinge of envy resurfaced.

"You can put your stuff anywhere you'd like, then come on up, and I'll show you around the helm," Kate called down.

Allie tossed her backpack and gear on the couch. "Enjoy the ride, Dad." She patted the urn and headed up the small stairway.

"Have a seat," Kate said from behind the steering wheel as she activated one of four large computer screens. She motioned to the empty black leather chair beside her with a tilt of her head. "I have the wreck's coordinates preprogramed into the computer." She pressed an icon on the screen.

"What are all these?" Allie referenced several more icons as the remaining three screens came to life.

"I can monitor every inch of this boat from here. If I press this." Kate pointed. "I can toggle between all the cameras. This one lets me know what's going on in the engine room, this is the AC settings, this controls the boat's onboard water supply, and this one..." Kate pressed the icon, and a grid of the boat appeared. "Are the lights. If I'm out on the water at night, I can dim them enough so they don't distract from my view of the stars."

"Very impressive." The one and only time Allie had been out on a boat at night had been a catamaran dinner cruise in San Francisco Bay. A birthday gift from one of her exes and a moment in time that had left a lasting impression.

"This screen," Kate continued, "lets you know where we are, where we're going, and everything that's happening in the water around and below us. I'll set the speed at thirteen knots. That'll get us there at a nice pace, and in the meantime"—she hit a button on the screen and glanced to Allie—"I'm going to put her on autopilot while I grab our breakfast. No other boats are in the area, so there shouldn't be any issues, but keep a lookout just in case, and holler if you see anything." Kate stood. "Be right back."

Allie settled deeper into her chair as the boat churned through the water. Okay, maybe she would rethink her mantra of *who needs wealth when one is rich at heart*. Because this sure beat the hell out of her lifestyle. But then again, why chase something unobtainable? No, she would not follow in her father's footsteps and let what she didn't have eat away at her soul. Still, having a new car, an apartment in a safer neighborhood, and the ability to give her mom some luxuries wouldn't suck. She folded her arms behind her head and watched the displays on the gauges move in different shapes and sizes as the GPS kept close tabs on their location. A rather large cluster of dots appeared on the one screen, and she guessed it was either a pod of dolphins or school of fish. For a brief moment, she wanted to jump overboard and check out the aquatic life surrounding the boat. To take a moment and be one with a world that she related to more than Kate's.

"And here we are," Kate said as she returned with a tray containing a burrito cut in half, two muffins, cut fruit, and two glasses of orange juice. "Mila made her signature breakfast burrito, and it's always big enough to feed three people."

"Mila made all that for just you?"

"Yeah. And there's more in the cooler. She keeps telling me I need to fatten up." Kate placed the tray between them, grabbed one of the burrito halves, and bit in.

"Well, eating all that would be a good start." Allie snatched the other half, took a bite, and moaned. "I really need to get some of her recipes. If I could cook like this, I'd probably be able to save my family's restaurant."

"That bad, huh?"

"Let's just say, it's been on life support for years." Allie began painting a detailed description of the day-to-day life of a run-down old diner with an equally aged out clientele. She settled into a comfortable monologue with Kate as she ate her breakfast and shared a condensed version of her life. Kate chimed in from time to time when Allie touched on the topic of her dad, and she realized that no matter how rich or poor a person was, most families had their share of some form of crazy.

"That's kinda the real reason I'm here. When I was a kid, my dad used to tell me this story about a tribe of people who—"

The pinging sound coming from the computer interrupted her.

"Hold that thought." Kate powered down on the throttle and slowed the yacht to a crawl. "We're here."

A twinge of excitement flushed through Allie. She had heard others talk enthusiastically about wreck diving, and she'd mentally placed it on her ever-expanding bucket list of all the things she'd wanted to do in her life but could never afford. She watched Kate maneuver the yacht in place, hit several buttons, and announce that they'd landed.

"So?" Kate raised a brow. "Did you enjoy the ride?"

"Are you kidding? I've never been on a yacht in my entire life. This thing's awesome."

"Yeah, it kinda is," Kate said with a hint of pride.

Allie leaned over the side. The water was a clear turquoise color, and the remains of the aircraft several yards away were visible. Kate stood next to her, reigniting the spark from the slightest touch of her skin.

"Rumor has it that this plane was part of a drug smuggling operation that was big here in the seventies. There're other planes and boat wrecks scattered around the Bahamas that are more popular with divers. The most famous being the wrecks from a couple James Bond movies that were filmed here, but I like diving at this one better."

"Oh yeah, why's that?"

"Because this one isn't such a tourist attraction like the others. And when I dive, I like fewer people around."

Allie scanned the area. They were the only ones at the site. In fact, they were the only ones in the area, so Kate definitely got her wish for solitude.

"Come on, you'll love it."

They grabbed their gear, both strapped a knife to their calf, and headed to the platform at the stern of the ship. "Here, wear these." Kate tossed her a pair of gloves. "The wreck is torn up and rusty. If you feel the need to reach out and touch anything, these'll keep you from a nasty cut that would attract unwelcome guests."

"Good idea. Thanks." Allie slid her fingers into the thick material. They felt a bit clunky as she wiggled her fingers but better that than the alternative.

"Ready?" Kate turned to her and smiled.

"Ready." Allie gave a thumbs-up as the two of them leaped off the platform and into the ocean. A momentary chill slapped the breath out of her, but it didn't take long for her body to adjust to the temperature as she began treading water.

"Okay." Kate swam in front of her. "Relaxation is the key to free diving. You'll need to take deep, slow, calm breaths and lower your heart rate. Try it. Breathe in for five seconds and out for ten."

Allie's pulse had been accelerated since she'd boarded the boat, but she knew it had nothing to do with nerves of freediving. She inhaled and exhaled several times and told herself to get a grip. She was wreck diving with Kate, not diving into her bed. She lightheartedly chuckled to herself and took a few more breaths until she felt her heart rate slow. She nodded to Kate.

"Calm?"

"Yeah, I think so."

"Good. Now then, do you have any idea how long you can hold your breath?"

"I don't know. About a minute or so, I guess." But truthfully, she had no clue. As a kid, she would pretend she was Aquaman and splash around her parents' porcelain tub while holding her breath. As an adult, when she had a stressful day or was going through a heartache, she would again draw a bath and completely immerse herself in a world that helped block out all the realities weighing on her. She'd stay underwater as long as possible, and when her chest felt like it was going to explode, she only surfaced enough of her face to take a breath before submerging again.

"Wow, a minute, that's great. And you've never free dived before?"

Allie shook her head. "When you date the co-owner of a dive shop, it's all about staying down and not surfacing until the tank runs out."

"Gotcha. Well, you're in for a treat. Ready?"

"Ready."

"I'll keep an eye on you. Let me know if something's up. I use the same hand signals as scuba."

Allie nodded, and she began her descent. About halfway down, she pinched her nose and exhaled until the pressure discomfort building in her ears subsided. Kate swam beside her and flashed a thumbs-up. She returned the signal and followed it with the okay sign. Kate smiled as she rolled upside down, extended her arms over her head and kicked like a dolphin as she effortlessly glided through the water, her long fins gracefully moving up and down, and her stomach muscles contracting with each stroke.

Watching her like that fulfilled all of Allie's lesbian mermaid fantasies, and she kicked with more force until she was over Kate's body. She matched her pace, and for a brief moment the two of them were in complete tandem as they defied gravity in a world that never failed to mesmerize her. She locked eyes with Kate, the two of them gazing through their masks at each other until Allie's lungs began beating on her chest, and she had to mentally control the gag reflex that was causing her to choke. She pointed toward the sky and rapidly ascended. Kate followed, and when they broke the surface, Allie gasped for air.

"Are you okay?"

Allie nodded as she coughed a few times. "I think I pushed my limits on that one."

"Do you want to go back to the boat, or are you still good?"

"No, no, I'm good. I just need a minute to catch my breath."

"Well, we're not that far from the wreck, we could snorkel the remaining distance, if you want?"

Allie shook her head. "No, I'm loving the feeling of being down there without being strapped to a tank. I just need to pace myself. I'll be fine."

"Take your time and go back down when you're ready. I'll be right beside you. You're doing great."

Three breaths later, she was back down enjoying the silent world and the closest sensation she would ever have of free flight. True to her word, Kate stayed by her side the entire time. She had to surface twice more before they made it to the wreck, and as annoying as that was, she had to admit there was something very freeing about this expression of diving. No bubbles meant less disruption of the water around her, and in turn, she was rewarded with up close and personal encounters with the abundant sea life that called the wreck home.

The propeller plane was in a state of decay. The wings were still attached, but the top of the fuselage was completely gone. Rust was eroding what was left, and an overgrowth of a variety of coral and sponges clung to the steel in an effort to transform the man-made device into one of the ocean's own.

They remained at the aircraft for about thirty minutes, surfacing for breaths when needed. The wreck wasn't anything spectacular, just an old plane on the floor of the ocean. But there was something ghostly enchanting about exploring a relic of the past that sat frozen in time. She wondered about the story behind the plane and thought once again about her father. The ocean didn't care about the history, stories, or heroics associated with the vessels that were housed in its world. Those were for humans to keep alive, embellish, and pass on.

"What did you think?" Kate said as they returned to the yacht and climbed aboard.

"I think I'm wondering where free diving has been all my life."

Kate tossed Allie a beach towel. "Careful, it becomes addictive."

"I think I'm already hooked."

"Well, welcome to the club." Kate handed Allie a glass of lemonade with a tilt of her head, conveying they should head toward the lounge chairs at the stern of the boat.

"Thanks, Kate, that was really wonderful." Allie settled into the soft cushion. A morning that had started out full of disappointment was shaping up to be one of the most enjoyable days she's had in a long time.

"I'm glad you liked it."

"More than liked it, I loved it. Thank you for inviting me."
Allie took a sip and subtly smacked her lips. For someone who
had never been overly fond of lemonade, she had to admit, the
touch of lavender offset the sweet-and-sour drink perfectly. "So
what's behind the name *Flyin' Free*?"

"It's in reference to a book where the main character is in
a wheelchair but stumbles across a magical spell that gives her
the ability to fly. It was a favorite of someone I once knew, and
I'd thought it made the perfect name for the yacht."

"That's a cool concept. The story sounds wonderful."

"Yeah," Kate said in a faraway voice. "She was." A blink
later, Kate turned her gaze to Allie. "I mean, it is. Anyway."
She waved a hand. "So, um, I was thinking. Would you like to
come up to the house and have dinner with me tonight? We can
sit on the patio and stargaze. Plus, as you know, I make a killer
lemonade." She referenced her drink in hand. "So drinks are on
me."

The invitation took her breath away. Being out on Kate's
yacht was an unexpected treat, but being asked to dinner? It was
hard not to read into the implications those words represented.
Or at least, what she hoped they did. "I'd love to," she said in
a calm smooth tone that in no way hinted at the excitement she
was feeling inside.

"How about five thirty?"

"Splendid." She cringed at how pretentious that sounded.
Splendid? Really? When had she ever used *that* word? Never.
She rolled her eyes in a moment of awkwardness, nestled
deeper into the chair, and let the sun warm her skin. Never in
her wildest fantasies had she ever imagined being on a yacht,
sharing a drink with a gorgeous woman, and with a romantic
stargazing evening yet to come. She flopped her head to her
side. Kate had her eyes closed, chin tilted to the sun, looking

relaxed and sexy as hell. It was one of those times in her life when Allie wished she had to power to suspend time and let the moment last forever.

But as she rolled her head back and closed her eyes, she sadly reminded herself that like most things in her life, the magic was temporary, the moment was fleeting, and the illusion of forever was just a dream. In a few days, they would both return to their realities that were worlds apart in more ways than one.

❖

"Knock, knock" Carla announced as she waltzed into Kate's house carrying a covered bamboo tray. "Where do you want this?"

"Thanks, Carla. Could you put it inside on the table?" Kate motioned without tearing her eyes from the ocean. It was another warm and beautiful evening, and a blanket of stars was beginning to light up the clear night sky.

"Sure thing." The sound of Carla's flip-flops faded away, then quickly returned. "You know, it's okay to feel something for someone else."

"What?" Kate glanced over as Carla sat next to Gizmo.

"Don't play coy with me. I saw you two when you got back from wreck diving, and I watched the way you looked at her and she at you. I've known you long enough to read you. You like her, and you know what, boss, there's nothing wrong with that."

"Okay, so you might be right. Maybe I am a little attracted to her." Kate reluctantly admitted. There was only one other time in her life when she'd come face-to-face with someone who had instantly ignited a spark from a deep gut level.

"Well, hot damn, it's about time you found love again."

"It's not love, Carla. Maybe an uptick of lust, but let's be clear about that."

"Okay fine, whatever. The point is, your emotions are flowing again with that wonderful tingly feeling." Carla shook her body like a belly dancer as she emphasized the word *tingly*.

"Wow, you, um, you look like you're enjoying this."

"I'm happy to see you happy again."

Kate sighed. "That's just it. I am happy, and yes, I do have those tingly feelings for Allie, but having feelings for her also makes me feel so goddamn guilty."

Carla bent over her knees and faced Kate. "Stop that. This isn't about replacing Brooke. This is about giving someone else a chance to make their own mark on your heart. It's not a competition. I think we both know Brooke will always take center stage. But your heart is big enough for more than one person to shine in that spotlight."

Maybe. Kate shrugged. The void in her heart hurt so much because Brooke had filled up the entire space. And even though time had numbed her pain, it hadn't erased it. But maybe there was an untouched part that was still available for someone else.

"I'm just saying. You are a wonderful person, boss, it would be a shame for you to live the rest of your life alone."

"I'm not alone. I have you and the staff, and new guests arrive every other week."

"You're alone in the place that matters the most."

"I don't need a lecture, Carla." She hated it when Carla pointed out the obvious about her. Mostly because she was always right.

"No, you don't." Carla rose and started to leave. "You need to love again."

"But—"

She held up her hand, silencing Kate. "I don't want a rebuttal. I have a right to my opinion. And by the way, I took

Gretta out this morning, and I could swear I heard Brooke hootin' and hollerin' as though she was sitting behind me. Maybe she's getting tired of something she loved so much sitting around doing nothing but collecting dust. Or someone." Carla emphasized the point as she leaned in and stared. Kate started to say something else, and again, Carla held up her hand. "I'm going, 'cause that's all I've got to say. And don't bother getting up, I know my way out."

"When do I ever get up?" She chuckled as Carla left. "Love you, Carla."

"Uh-huh."

Kate never had someone she could anoint with the title of best friend. Granted, she had a lot of people in her orbit. In fact, one text announcing she was going to a bar could summon upward of two dozen people to join her. Her social media page kept a daily running tally of how many friends she had, as though that number held some sort of truth behind it. But after she became clean and sober, most dropped out of her life, seemingly too busy to go out for a coffee and talk her through the demons that were still trying to pull her down.

None of them would have slept in a lounge chair by her side in case she needed someone to talk to after waking from a nightmare, bring her and Gizmo food throughout the day, make her take a shower, or at least force her to walk into the ocean for a dip. Much less run the resort, pick up the guests, and make sure that her world, although falling apart from the inside, would not crumble on the outside. And to do it all with a smile and never once ask for anything in return.

"You know she's right," the soft voice in her head confirmed. Kate glanced at the lounge chair that only moments ago held Carla and saw Brooke sitting there smiling at her.

"Oh, now you're taking her side, are you?"

"This isn't about sides, my love, this is about happiness." The image of Brooke got up and walked the short distance and sat next to her.

She cupped Kate's face, and Kate leaned her chin into Brook's hands. "I miss you so much."

"Oh, baby, I'm always right here." Brooke repositioned her hand over Kate's heart. "But what I can no longer give you, she can."

"I…can't…have feelings for anyone but you," Kate choked out. "It just doesn't feel right."

"But don't you see, you already do. Embrace it and be as happy for yourself as I am for you." Brooke leaned in. "You have always been a free spirit, my love. Your wings were never meant to be clipped." She stood, tilted her head to the sky, and stretched out her arms. "What a beautiful night to stargaze. Don't you just want to reach out and hug the sky?"

Kate chuckled as she watched Brooke close her arms around herself in a tight embrace. "You always had a way with—"

"Kate?" Allie's soft voice interrupted as she approached. "Is this a bad time? Are you on the phone? You told me to let myself in."

Kate glanced over. "Wow, you look, um…" She wanted to say sexy. Not that seeing Allie in her diving attire and relaxed beach wear wasn't, but the combination of tight black jeans, formal shirt, makeup, and styled hair was definitely a package that was holding her attention and waking her desires. "Nice." She cringed as she finished her thoughts on a word that fell short of describing Allie's true beauty.

"Thank you." Allie displayed a shy coyness as she averted her eyes and smiled.

Kate hopped out of her chair. "Are you hungry?"

"Starving," Allie said as she sat with Gizmo on the lounge chair and started rubbing her under the chin.

"Then you came to the right place. You stay here and continue spoiling Giz while I go make us a plate."

Kate hurried into the kitchen, bent forward, placed her hands on her knees, and took several deep breaths. After a beat, she slowly straightened and pressed her back against the wall. Before she became clean and sober, entertaining the thought of being with someone would have been a no-brainer. In fact, by this time into the "date," she was usually half-numb, and all the filters of her behavior were well past the self-conscious part. She'd wanted a good time, and she'd wanted to get off, and that was about the extent of how far-reaching her feelings went. Remembering the person's name or the actual details of the lovemaking was inconsequential.

Brooke was the first woman she had been with clean and sober, and it was an eye-opening experience. To touch and be touched by another and actually remember what it felt like instead of flashes of memories? To care, for the first time ever, if the other person was pleased with the acts she performed on her instead of just powering through the motions? With Brooke, she was not only introduced to the beauty of sober lovemaking, she was reintroduced to herself. To feelings of love she had shoved into a dark corner of her soul because she'd learned at an early age that they were too painful and made her feel too vulnerable to bring into the light.

And now, for the second time in her life, she was becoming both bashful and excited about the thought of touching and being touched. To teeter on that ledge of feeling loved and vulnerable in another's arms. She took a deep breath. Was she really ready for what this night would probably bring? No, but she had learned that timing, whether good or bad, was something that was never in one's control. She peeled herself off the wall and approached the tray of food Mila had prepared. A small piece of paper was sticking out from under the one plate.

Kate freed it and smiled. *I hope my cooking is the second-best thing of your evening.*

Good old Mila, the woman was as gruff as an old barn cat on the outside but at times, could be as soft as a teddy bear on the inside. But she was getting old, and Kate worried more and more about her. Too bad every time she suggested Mila hire an assistant, the claws came out, and a look of hurt shrouded her face. The kitchen was her throne, and the meals and recipes she created were her stamp on her kingdom. "The moment you bring someone else in here," she would say, "is the moment I walk out." She would not be dethroned by, "Some uppity young person who doesn't know their ass from an acai berry."

Kate took the lids off the bowls and basket of rolls, placed two glasses of lemonade on the tray and waltzed back to the patio. "And here we are." She placed the tray on the table and dragged another lounge chair closer to hers. "You'll be more comfortable with a chair of your own." Allie took a seat as Kate handed her a plate. "Formal dining isn't a thing here. I hope you don't mind?"

"Not at all." Allie dug her fork deep into the creamy noodles. "Oh my God." She moaned as she chewed. "This is delicious."

"Well, I wish I could take credit, but I haven't made a meal since Mila started working here. She gets insulted if I eat anything she hasn't prepared herself."

"This pasta is the best I think I've ever had."

"Well, I can tell you all I know about the dish. It's mushroom stroganoff. The sauce is cashew based with onions and leeks, and of course, it's sprinkled with Mila's mix of special spices."

"The woman really is gifted." Allie said.

They settled into a comfortable chitchat as they enjoyed their dinner, Gizmo happily oinking by Kate's side as she ate the bowl of cut fruit and vegetables Mila had prepared for her.

After all plates were empty, Kate presented her phone. "And now for tonight's entertainment. Stargazing. Get your phone out."

Allie did as she was instructed.

"Download this app." She presented her screen.

Allie nodded. "Okay, now what?"

With a tap, Kate opened the app and pointed her phone to the sky. Allie did the same, and it was like having a planetarium in the palms of their hands, complete with the names of stars and constellations.

"There's Orion." Kate excitedly pointed. "And Pegasus... oh, and The Big Dipper," she said as she swept her phone slowly through the air.

"I've never done this before. How accurate is it?"

Kate shrugged. "Don't know, and since I have no clue about astronomy, I'm going to assume it's spot-on. And look." Kate leaned over. "If you hit this icon, it'll show you the image of whatever the constellation was named after."

Allie tapped her screen, swept her phone to the left and snorted. "What ancient astronomer thought *that* cluster of stars looked like a bull?"

"What? Where are you?"

"Over there." Allie pointed. "By Orion."

Kate moved her phone a bit until she zeroed in on Taurus. She smiled. Brooke used to say the same thing about the imagination of the Greek astronomers.

"What sign are you?" Allie asked.

"Cancer."

Allie swept her phone in a slow circle until she found the constellation and giggled. "I hate to break it to you, but your five dots look nothing like a crab."

"What are you?"

"I'm an Aries."

"Aries," Kate said as she searched. "Oh, and look who's talking. Four dots that basically look like a straight line. I don't see the makings of a ram in there anywhere." She chuckled.

"Yeah, I'd say the ancient astronomers definitely...look!" Allie pointed. "A shooting star."

"Make a wish."

They paused, and instead of a wish, Kate silently thanked the universe for bringing someone as special as Allie into her life.

"You know," Allie said as she broke the silence. "When I was a kid, my father used to tell me a story about a tribe of Polynesian people who lived peacefully on an island until a ship of traders came and decided they wanted to call the land theirs. A last-stand battle took place, and between fishing spears and guns, you can guess how the story ends. My dad said the sky shed tears in the form of shooting stars that night as it mourned." Allie gazed at Kate. "His side of the family always believed they were direct descendants of those people."

"Really?"

"Yeah, but here's the twist in the story. I took a DNA test in high school that debunked the whole thing. None of it's real. Come to find out, our family mix of DNA soup doesn't contain a single drop of Polynesian. So my dad's family story about our ancestors was nothing more than a tall tale. But I never told him that."

"Why not?"

"Because he loved to believe he was something he wasn't. In fact, that's actually the real reason why I'm here. My dad died a few months ago and—"

"I'm so sorry."

"Thanks." Allie flashed a smile. "His dying request was to have his urn buried in the same spot where the supposed last 'battle' on the merchant ship took place. And here's the second plot twist to the story. My dad got the coordinates from a tribal 'ancestor' who appeared and spoke to him in a dream."

"You're kidding," Kate said, amused.

"I'm not. And those coordinates just happen to be right out there, miles away from anywhere remotely Polynesian." She pointed. "Guess the ancestor in his dream didn't have access to Google Maps." She giggled at her own joke. "Anyway, I was going to bury him this morning, but as you know, those plans were a bit derailed."

Shit. Allie's words were like a punch to Kate's gut. Bury her father? Seriously? "So, um," she stumbled as feelings of guilt surfaced. "The whole treasure hunting thing really—"

"Was, as I showed you last night, never the reason why I came here," Allie interrupted. "Although, when I was down there checking out a spot to bury dad, I did stumble upon an old Timex watch sticking out of the sand, so maybe I'm missing out on something."

They shared a lighthearted laugh.

"Seriously, though. I haven't used the metal detector. I'm not a treasure hunter. I'm just a daughter who's here to bury her father in a place he believed would reunite his soul with a group of fictitious ancestors. And as batshit crazy as that sounds, who am I to deny him his last wish? Or so my mother keeps reminding me."

Kate averted her eyes as a feeling of shame settled over her. Not only had she not believed Allie, but her paranoia had denied a father's dying wish. "That's, um, wow, that's very nice of you."

"Well, don't go singing my praises. Initially, I didn't want to do it. I wanted the money spent on this adventure to go to my mom for necessary repairs around the house and restaurant. She's the one who talked me into it. I'm here because of a promise I made to her, and once I get the boat up and running again, I'll bury his urn, fulfill the wish, and that'll be that. Even though there's no truth to the family story, at least Dad picked a beautiful location to be laid to rest." She titled her head toward Kate. "And I met you."

Allie's words tingled through Kate's body and for the moment overshadowed the overwhelming feeling she had of being a total ass. "Tell you what." Step one in correcting one's mistake, as taught by her father, was never admit fault. Instead, throw out a distraction while others fixed the issue behind the scenes. She'd send Carla a text as soon as she could and have her reverse the sabotage, meanwhile… "Tomorrow, I'll have Carla look at your boat. She knows her way around a car engine, so she'll probably able to figure it out. I'm sure it's something simple. Meanwhile, I'll make you an offer. We can take the yacht out first thing in the morning. I can raid Mila's kitchen and grab enough food so we can make a sunrise breakfast, and you can bury your father's urn. Afterward, we can do some more diving, or I can show you around some other places not too far from here that are beautiful. We could even go to Exuma and hang out on pig beach."

"Are you serious?" Allie's eyes widened.

"Very. So what do you say?"

"Are you kidding. Yes, of course, yes. But only on one condition," she said with enthusiasm.

"Oh?" Kate cocked her head.

"If you let me cook for you. I'm no Mila, but I do have a few tricks up my sleeve."

"Deal." Allie was adorable when she was excited, and for a moment, Kate thought about leaning over and kissing her. But ever since Allie had broken the news of why she was really on the island, her early thoughts of the possibility of the evening ending in her bedroom had been replaced with the buzzkill of remorse and anxiety. She really needed to talk to Carla and make things right.

"What time should I meet you?"

"How about being at the yacht at six."

"That'll…" Allie yawned and covered her mouth. "Oh my gosh, sorry about that, I guess I still haven't caught up on my sleep."

"We can make it later if—"

"No, no. A sunrise breakfast at sea is a bucket list invitation. Six o'clock is perfect." She stretched. "In fact, it's getting late, and I should probably get going since it'll be another early morning." She stood. "Thank you for such a gracious offer and for such a lovely evening. Can I help clean up?"

Kate waved her off. "Nah. Gizmo's my little garbage disposal. I give the leftovers to her."

"Well, if I knew that, I wouldn't have eaten so much."

"It's a good thing you did. Giz needs to lose some weight, huh, sweetie?" She bent and scratched Gizmo on the head as she grunted.

"Well, thanks again, Kate. I had a really nice time," Allie said in a soft voice as she opened her arms.

At first, the embrace felt a little awkward, but soon, she sensed Allie relax as much as she had, and the good night hug quickly morphed into one of those embraces that felt like she was being wrapped in a warm and cozy blanket. She closed her eyes and inhaled the earthy undertones of Allie's perfume. Her senses came alive, and the feelings she was trying so hard to keep locked inside resurfaced. Her mind and heart were racing, and as she broke the moment between them and leaned back ever so slightly, Allie groaned.

The distance between their lips was just a few inches, and if Kate was reading the look in Allie's eyes correctly, a kiss would be welcome and mutual. She closed the distance and felt the warmth of Allie's breath as she moistened her lips and parted them in anticipation.

The sound of a loud crash startled them, and they jerked apart. The moment was lost as they both glanced at the shattered plate of food that Gizmo had nudged off the table.

"And this is why I keep telling Mila to put my food on plastic plates." Kate bent and picked up several pieces of broken plate that were dripping in sauce as Gizmo licked the tile.

"Can I help you with—"

"Nope, I got it." Kate scurried into the kitchen and returned with a dustpan. "We've had this happen before."

Allie took a few steps back. "Okay, then I'll let you do what you need to do, and I'll see you"—she playfully pointed to Kate—"in a few hours."

"You don't have to go, this will only take a minute," Kate said as she squatted over the mess and began sweeping up the scattered pieces.

"No, I think I should. Besides, tomorrow sounds like it'll be a full day."

"Would you like a ride back to your casita?" Kate glanced toward Allie as she began walking away.

Allie shook her head. "Nope, you finish what you're doing. I'd prefer to walk, but thanks anyway."

"Okay. Good night, Allie. And thanks for a wonderful night," she said as Allie twiddled her fingers over her shoulder and vanished around the corner.

Gizmo leaned in and nuzzled against her. Kate lost her balance and flopped to the floor.

"Oh no, you don't. After what you just did, don't you even think about cozying up to me. Consider yourself in the doghouse the rest of the night," Kate said as she rested her arms on her knees and stared at the corner of her house, willing Allie to return and finish what they had almost started.

But after a beat, she begrudgingly concluded that Allie was probably right. Tomorrow was going to be a full day. One that would begin with a lot of emotions for Allie. Maybe, Kate thought as she grumbled and lightheartedly scolded Giz for her awful timing, the night had ended exactly as it was meant to. She exhaled a heavy sigh as she finished her task, emptied the dustpan in the kitchen trash, and returned to the patio.

She grabbed her phone, hit Carla's number, and put her on speaker as she raised her binoculars and focused on Allie strolling down the beach back to the resort. At one point, Allie threw her arms out and twirled. Kate smiled. "Yeah," she said. "I feel the same way."

"Hey, boss, what's up?"

"Carla, do me a favor and reverse what you did to Allie's boat."

"Reverse it? Already? But I thought we decided—"

"She's not a treasure hunter."

"How do you know?"

"She's here to bury her dad's urn in the ocean. It's why she rented the boat, so she could sail out to certain coordinates where her dad wanted to be placed. And the metal detector came as a package deal when she rented her scuba gear."

"Bury her dad? Wow, I never would have guessed that one."

"Me, neither. Look, she'll be with me all morning. I offered to take the yacht out and help her bury him. I anticipate we'll be gone until late afternoon. I already told her I'd have you look over her boat to see if you could fix it. You good with that?"

"Yeah, boss, no worries. I'll handle it. In fact, you want me to do it now?"

"No, no. Tomorrow will be fine." She probably should have told Carla to reverse the sabotage that night, but selfishly, she was enjoying having Allie all to herself, and she was looking forward to another full day with her. What she'd done was a shit move in hindsight, but it had unexpectedly opened a door to a part of her heart that she had seemed hell-bent on keeping closed. "And thanks, I owe you one."

"You know, I've always been very fond of your underwater scooter."

"Bye, Carla." Kate chuckled as she disconnected the call and placed the phone and binoculars on the table. She returned to her chair, clasped her fingers behind her head, and gazed at the stars. She felt lighter than she had felt in years, and for the first time in a long time, a new face was taking up a lot of space in her mind.

❖

"Ahoy there, and do I smell coffee?" Allie stood on the dock toward the stern of the yacht as she waited for permission to board.

"Ahoy, and yes you do." After a restless night of trying to calm her woken and aroused body, Kate was up at four, raiding Mila's kitchen by four-thirty, and was relaxing under the soft glow of her yacht's preset romantic lighting mode by five. She was sipping her third cup of coffee when Allie arrived. "What do you say we get your gear transferred over, then I'll pour you a cup."

"Sounds like a plan."

Kate hopped off her yacht, and the urge to hug Allie good morning was overshadowed with the desire to get out to sea and enjoy a sunrise breakfast with her.

"Now, then." Allie jumped on her boat and grabbed a cylinder. "If you could take this"—she grunted as she held it out to Kate—"I'll grab my gear bag."

In a motion that looked synchronized and rehearsed, they danced around each other as they stowed Allie's gear, untied the mooring lines, and headed to the helm.

"Let's get her outta the lagoon, and then I'll get you that cup of coffee. What are your coordinates?"

Allie activated her phone and read off the numbers as Kate punched them into the yacht's computer, even though Kate already knew the approximate location.

"Thanks again for doing this. I really appreciate it."

"No problem. It's the least I can do. Oh, and I talked to Carla last night, and she said she'd look over your boat today, so I'm confident it'll be up and running in no time. Carla's a whiz at fixing things."

"Thank you. Olivia swears she thoroughly looked it over before she rented it to me." Allie shrugged.

"Well, it looks like she's seen better days, and things do happen." Kate swallowed another lump of guilt stuck in her throat. Carla would reverse the battery cable today, all would be well, and Allie would never know the embarrassing truth of her behavior. She let out a sigh, settled into her seat, and threw out her own form of an apology. "Wanna steer?"

"What? Are you kidding? You would trust me with this thing?"

"Anyone who can navigate that beat-up old boat from Nassau can definitely take this one a few hundred yards out. I'll keep it off autopilot. Just use this screen to guide you."

Allie displayed her phone, and it pinged their location in relation to the coordinates.

"Or that." Kate chuckled. "I'll go grab us that coffee. Cream, sugar? What's your poison?"

"Don't suppose you've got almond or soy milk?"

"Almond."

"Perfect. Just splash a bit in there, and I'll be happy."

Kate slid out of her seat and let Allie take over. "Why don't you set the speed at thirteen knots? That'll get us there at a nice pace, and we'll still have plenty of time for a sunrise breakfast."

"Sounds good."

"And don't forget, these screens are your eyes. Especially during night navigation."

"Yep, got it."

Allie throttled forward as Kate placed a hand on her shoulder. "I'll be right back." She shimmied down the ladder to the main section of the boat and headed to the kitchen. She poured two fresh mugs of coffee, topped both off with a splash of almond milk, and within a minute, was back at the helm.

She placed Allie's mug in a holder and settled back into her chair as she took a sip. She resisted the urge to be a back seat driver when thoughts like...*are you checking the screens?* Or, *you're a little over thirteen knots, bring her back down,* formed at the tip of her lips. Instead, she exhaled her anxieties and concentrated on enjoying the ride with a beautiful woman by her side, one who hadn't broken the smile that creased her face the moment Kate had told her she could take the wheel. Allie was like watching a wide-eyed child at a magic show, and her apparent joy was infectious.

When the computer notified them that they were getting close to the location, Allie slowed the boat and with the help of Kate, killed the engine when they were in place. "Where's the anchor?"

"Right here." Kate leaned over and let her touch linger on Allie's hand as she hit a button. "So," she said. "What'd ya think?"

"Are you kidding? You were right yesterday when you said yachting doesn't suck."

"Yeah, she's an awesome boat," Kate said with pride. "Are you hungry?"

"I am."

"The sun will be up in about thirty minutes. Whaddaya say we make breakfast, then sit on the deck and watch the sunrise?"

"Sounds good." Allie grabbed her mug and followed Kate into the galley.

"There's fruit, vegetables, eggs, and potatoes in the basket. Spices are in here." Kate opened a cabinet. "Pots and pans in there, and plates and utensils over here." She pointed.

"Perfect, now." Allie shooed her with a wave of her hand. "You go away, relax, and let me do my thing."

Kate topped off her coffee, flopped in one of the lounge chairs on the stern, and let her body relax. She loved being out at sea at daybreak. The sound of lapping water against the boat, the slight rocking motion, and the hint of pastel colors forming on the horizon all added up to a sense of tranquility she had yet to duplicate anywhere else. She took another sip and pushed deeper into the cushion as her senses perked up at the tantalizing aroma wafting in the air. Damn, that smelled good. Her stomach began to grumble a bit, and she fought back the urge to go into the kitchen and sample the food. No, she thought, better let Allie do her thing. Besides, patience would make it taste that much better. Twenty minutes later, she heard soft footsteps approach.

"Ready for breakfast?"

"Mmm, it smells delicious." Kate swung her feet over the side of her chair as Allie placed two plates on the table between them. "Do you need me to refresh your mug?"

"No, I'm good, but thank you."

Kate glanced down at the food. "Wow, this looks amazing." She grabbed her fork and dug into the omelet the size of her plate. The stringy mozzarella mixed with sautéed vegetables melted in her mouth in a savory bite of sheer deliciousness. "Oh my God, this is amazing," she moaned.

"Well, thank you. I know it's not as good as Mila's, but I'd like to think I've mastered a few unique flavors of my own."

"Yeah, she's the best, but trust me, this rivals her." Kate settled back into her chair and brought her plate with her. "I don't mean to be rude, but I want to watch the sunrise as we eat."

Allie did the same, and they fell into a comfortable silence as nature dazzled them for the next thirty minutes with her palette of brilliant deep-hued oranges and reds. As soon as the blush colors morphed into a pale baby blue, Allie stood and announced it was probably time to head into the water.

They put their plates in the kitchen, and Kate helped Allie with her tank. "What else do you need?"

Allie checked her respirator. "Would you mind handing me my backpack? Oh, and I'll need the shovel in the gear bag."

Kate did as she was instructed, and as Allie retrieved the urn, Kate couldn't help but notice her prolonged and frozen stare at the container. She approached and rubbed her hand across her shoulder. "I'm so sorry."

"You know, my father and I were never close," Allie said in a faraway voice. "I mean, there were moments, but overall, we were oil and water." She turned. "I guess it's hitting me harder than I thought it would. Holding his ashes, knowing that I'm about to say a final good-bye to him feels surprisingly painful."

Kate thought about her father and the Grand-Canyon-sized gap in their relationship. He was nothing more than a figurehead. A person with the title of Dad that designated him legally responsible for her physical well-being, but nowhere in the contract of parental obligations did it mention tending to her emotional health or nurturing love. That duty—hell, who was she kidding, all the parental duties—were farmed out to others to fulfill. If he died tomorrow, would she honestly feel any pain?

"If you want to do this by yourself, I—"

"No." Allie's reply was immediate. "I'd really like you to join me."

Those words warmed Kate's heart, and she approached Allie at the edge of the platform. Allie paused, stared into the water, filled her lungs, then nodded. They jumped in together, did a final adjustment of their own gear, and when Allie gave the thumbs-up, Kate flanked her as they descended to a cluster of three boulders.

Kate settled next to her on bent knees, and as Allie began digging a hole, she glanced around. There was no coral, seagrass, or anything that would add a touch of beauty to this final resting spot. Just a pile of large rocks, bare sand, and turquoise ocean for as far as her eyes could see. It wasn't much to look at, but it held a serenity that exceeded any cemetery Kate had ever been to. When she returned her gaze to Allie, she had already placed the urn in the hole and was leaning over it in what Kate interpreted as Allie saying her final piece to her father. A beat later, Allie covered the urn with sand, and as the disturbed sediment danced with the sun's rays, it sparkled around them in a magical display of floating glitter. Allie's lips were turned up, her arms outstretched, and a look of wonder graced her eyes. Nature had given Allie's father the perfect send-off.

Kate stayed next to her until the last particle of sand settled, and her chest began pounding the warning that she was reaching the last of her oxygen reserves. She rested her hand on Allie's shoulder, and when Allie focused on her, she pointed up. Allie nodded, and they ascended at the same pace.

"You didn't have to surface with me. I just needed a breath." Kate gulped air as she treaded water.

Allie removed her regulator. "I know, but I'm done doing what I needed to do. If you don't mind, I think I'd like to just sit on your deck for the remainder of the morning and relax."

"Yeah, sure, that sounds great."

They snorkeled the short distance to the boat, and Kate helped Allie shed her gear once they were aboard. "How about a drink?" she said as she shook the water from her hair, tossed Allie a beach towel, and shuffled toward the kitchen. "I brought a jug of lemonade."

"You wouldn't by chance have anything a little stronger to add to it?"

"No, sorry. I gave that up when it became clear it was robbing me of my life. But if you need to take the edge off, I can offer you something that's even better than booze. Come on." She tilted her head as she grabbed two glasses of lemonade. She led Allie to the stern of the boat, hit a button, and a section of the floor slid open, exposing a small round Jacuzzi.

"You've got to be kidding me? You have a Jacuzzi on your yacht?"

"Well, I couldn't really turn it down. It was part of the package." She stepped into the warm water, placed the glasses in separate holders, hit a button, and settled into one of four bubbling seats. "I find that a relaxing soak works wonders when it comes to taking the stress away." She leaned back, tipped her chin to the sun, closed her eyes, and let the jets pulse and massage her muscles. A moment later, she heard Allie stepping into the water, and she smiled.

"This is nice." Allie cooed as she settled into an opposite seat.

"Yes. It's another one of those perks that doesn't suck." Kate opened her eyes, focused on Allie, and could tell by her expression she was once again in a faraway place.

"My dad would have loved this. He always wanted to have so much more than what he had. My whole life, I watched him struggle in a battle he waged with himself. Mom told me that when they first opened the diner, he would see wealthy people and all their fancy cars and toys and say to her, one day, we're going to have a car like that. Or one day, we're going to have a house like that. All he could see were the things he didn't have instead of what he did."

Kate slid over and sat next to her. "Hey," she whispered as she tucked a wet strand of hair that was clinging to Allie's cheek behind her ear. "Fancy cars and boats don't always lead to happiness. I grew up in a bubble that was full of stuff but devoid of the thing I wanted the most, love. My dad is very obsessed with money and the power it wields. Don't get me wrong, wealth is nice." She referenced her surroundings. "But when you're a kid, there's so much more that matters."

"Seems as though we have something in common."

Kate ran her thumb gently over Allie's cheek. No, what they had in common was more intimate than emotionally unavailable fathers. Grief, regret, anger, and an entire mixed bag of other shitty feelings from a life that fell short of expectations. They were all manifestations of pain expressing themselves in different ways. And *that* was what they had in common.

Allie cupped Kate's hand and gently kissed it. "Thank you for being my knight in shining armor and giving me the perfect day for this," she whispered as she locked eyes with Kate.

They were gentle eyes, and in them, Kate saw a kindred soul. Allie leaned in, and as soon as their lips touched, she relished in the sensation of once again feeling flesh on flesh. Of releasing the pent-up energy that had been building since Allie had set foot on her island. And as her hunger grew, she repositioned herself over Allie and kissed her deeply.

"Are you okay with this?" she moaned in Allie's ear.

"More than okay," Allie whispered.

They let their tongues take center stage in a dance that readied Kate's body for what was yet to come. And even though the Jacuzzi's water was warm, her nipples were rock hard as Allie's fingers tickled and glided over them. "I want to—"

The hum of a propeller plane interrupted them. Kate leaned back, shielded her eyes, and squinted toward the sky. The placard on the plane identified it as a tourist charter, and it was flying low and heading in their direction.

"Let's take this to the bedroom." It wasn't a question but a summons, and Allie seemed to gladly obey as she took Kate's extended hand and followed her into the master suite. The room was at the bow of the ship, furnished with a cherry wood, king-size bed and nightstand combo, facing floor-to-ceiling windows that gave an unobstructed view of the ocean in the daylight and at night provided the sensation of floating on a blanket of stars. For a brief moment, Kate froze in the doorway as memories cascaded in her mind.

Allie seemed to sense this as she stepped next to her and snaked an arm around her waist. "You okay?"

If she was going to make love to Allie, she had to get Brooke out of her head, or it wouldn't be fair to either of them. She turned and searched Allie's eyes. They were a similar shade of brown to Brooke's, but they were Allie's eyes, and right now, they held a desire for her that was undeniable. She blinked away the past and in one swift motion, ushered in the present. She stepped in front of Allie, cupped her face, and kissed her deep as she slowly walked her toward the bed.

Kate reached behind Allie, unclasped her bikini top, and broke the kiss only to pull the stringed loop over her head before she reunited their tongues. The heavier Allie's breathing became, the more it turned Kate on, and when the wetness that emerged between her legs demanded attention, she lowered Allie to the bed. She straddled Allie's stomach and took a moment to glance at her small, perfect breasts. Her nipples were hard and pink, and Kate couldn't help but lick her lips in anticipation of what was to come.

"You're beautiful," she said as she refocused and gazed into Allie's eyes.

Allie raised her hands, gently pressed them against Kate's cheek, and began to pull her forward. But Kate upended those plans as she clasped Allie's wrists, slowly bringing them over Allie's head until she'd pinned her to the bed.

"You okay with this?" Kate's desires turned into an insatiable hunger that she hadn't felt in years as an urgency to have them satisfied took hold.

"Mm-hmm." Allie nodded as her breathing accelerated.

Kate released her grip as she repositioned herself and pressed her lips to Allie's breast and gently sucked on her nipple. Allie's moans filled her head and became increasingly intoxicating.

"Let's get out of these." Kate tugged at Allie's shorts, and they both took a moment to wiggle out of the last of their clothes before reuniting their bodies, fusing skin on skin and breast to breast. She shivered. Was there anything more beautiful than the touch of a woman's soft body? She raised up enough to let her breasts glide over Allie's before scooting down and wrapping her tongue around one nipple, then the other. They were hard and welcoming, and she fought the urge to lean back and glance at Allie's body. To sear the image of every inch of nakedness into her mind. Instead, she cupped Allie's breasts and moved her thumbs over the wet nipples, pinching them ever so gently. Allie arched her back.

Kate stopped her motion. "Too hard?"

Allie placed her hands over Kate's and manipulated them back to her breast. "It's perfect." She breathed the words down Kate's neck, triggering another shiver.

"I see." Kate leaned forward and demanded another tongue-locking kiss. She was so turned on right now, part of her wanted to flip their positions and have Allie relieve the ache pounding in her clit, but she didn't want to relinquish control. When she broke the kiss, she raised her upper body and leaned back on bent legs. She lowered herself onto Allie and began grinding gently. "You good?"

"Mm-hmm."

Kate reached down and reunited one hand with Allie's breasts as she placed the other on her own nipple and began massaging the ache that beckoned to be released.

"I can help with that." Allie replaced Kate's hand with her own.

"Yes," Kate whispered as she felt a rough pinch, then the softness of Allie's fingers rolling her flesh between them. "Yes," she repeated as the wetness pooled between her legs, and her own desires reached a fever pitch. She wanted to take Allie as much as she wanted to be taken. The dilemma to prolong the lovemaking and explore each other or to shift to raw, hard sex was Ping-Ponging in her mind. Another pinch to her nipple almost made her come as the urgency to satisfy her desires surfaced. She searched Allie's eyes for a clue as to how Allie would want to play. Allie tipped her head in a motion that beckoned to Kate.

Kate bent forward, leaning on outstretched arms until the words, "Let's come together," rose above their heavy breaths. She nodded as she drove her tongue deep into Allie's mouth and repositioned herself to her side, giving both a good angle and enough reach. She found Allie's fingers, clasped them, and slowly brought them to her wetness. She leaned out of the kiss and arched her back. Her other hand traveled down Allie's torso until she could tease Allie's wetness before entering her. Seconds later, she felt Allie do the same.

"You set the pace," Kate said through heavy breaths. "I'll match—"

Her thought was interrupted as she felt Allie's fingers dive deep inside her. She reciprocated, and as Allie increased the pace, stroking the walls within her, she did the same. She closed her eyes, pushed her body deeper onto Allie's fingers, and moved her hips to the rhythm. "Harder. Faster," she heard but wasn't sure if it was she or Allie giving the orders.

A pinch to her nipple caused her to open her eyes and focus. Allie smiled ever so slightly as she stroked Kate hard and fast, rolling her nipples with such precision, it was making Kate dizzy with pleasure. They moved on each other with accelerated pace, arms twisted around and between each other until Kate felt the familiar build begin. She rocked harder on Allie's fingers until the release in her throat came with the same intensity as her orgasm.

A moment later, she felt Allie tighten around her fingers and knew she'd gotten her wish. They slowed their bodies, and when Allie nodded, they removed their fingers in tandem.

Kate collapsed next to Allie with a thud and flopped onto her back. Both breathing heavy as beads of sweat appeared on their skin. They lay side by side until Kate's heart rate and body calmed enough for speech to return. "That…was amazing." She turned on her side and gave Allie a soft kiss on the cheek, then snuggled next to her.

"It was pretty amazing, huh?" Allie's voice was barely audible. "*You're* pretty amazing."

Kate planted another kiss on her cheek. Before this week, she hadn't imagined her heart would beat for anyone but Brooke. And now, as she lay with her head resting on Allie's chest and with the warmth of her skin pressed against hers, she was starting to wonder.

"I'm sorry again about your dad," she said as she trailed a finger gently around Allie's torso.

"Thanks." Allie settled her bent arm behind her head. "You know what's weird? I always loved my dad, but for most of my life, I didn't like him." She paused. "He wasn't the easiest or the best father, that's for sure, but as odd as this sounds, there's a part of me that's really going to miss him."

Kate rolled over on her back and stared at the ceiling in thought. "My dad didn't win any father of the year awards either. He was a womanizer, and I blamed him for my mom's never-ending substance abuse. Dealing with his shit was more than she could handle. A revolving door of nannies raised me because neither of them was around much physically or emotionally."

"You were raised by nannies?" Allie turned on her side and faced Kate.

"I, um, my real name isn't Kate Williams. It's Suzanne Bennett. I changed it years ago in an attempt to break away from my past and create a new life for myself. You may have heard of me."

Allie brought her first finger close to her thumb. "Just a little mention or two."

Kate chuckled as she grabbed Allie's hand, entwined their fingers, and brought them to her lips for a kiss. "Well, don't believe everything you read."

"What? You mean there's no truth in tabloid gossip?" Allie teased.

That confirmed to Kate that Allie had not only heard of her, but she'd probably seen the embarrassing photos as well. There was a part of her that felt like she should explain to Allie that she was a different person from her *Bad Girl Bennett* persona, but since Allie didn't ask a barrage of questions about what it was like to be the only heir to a billion-dollar empire, Kate gladly left it alone.

Allie snuggled closer and wrapped her body over Kate's. "Thanks for letting me know. And by the way, I don't care who you are. To me, you're someone who stepped up when I needed a hand at a time when I was feeling vulnerable. And for that, I'll always be grateful."

Kate forced a smile as the same twinge of guilt for the sabotage surged through her. Another of life's lessons learned, and unlike so many others, she hoped this one wouldn't come back and bite her in the ass.

❖

Kate jerked awake at the sound of another low-flying plane and craned her neck as she glanced around the room. Allie stirred in her arms as Kate focused on the clock on the wall. It was two thirty.

"I think I fell asleep." Allie yawned and stretched.

"We both did." Kate kissed her forehead as she peeled herself off the bed, got dressed, walked to the windows, and glanced out as the plane flew over. It was another private charter, and that made her pause. Normally, they flew over the wrecks, Pig Beach, or Staniel Cay. Seeing two in the area in one day made her annoyed at the thought that they were widening their sightseeing range. Her momentary invasion of privacy was interrupted as Allie came from behind and wrapped her arms around her waist.

"It's so beautiful," Allie said in a soft voice as she rested her chin on Kate's shoulder.

Kate nodded. Most nights, she fell asleep on her patio lounge chair, listening to the waves crash ashore and woke every morning to the sun glistening off the water. Nothing in her life had ever brought her soul to a state of peacefulness like the ocean.

She turned in Allie's arms and was leaning in to kiss her when her phone jingled. "Shit, that's Carla's ringtone. She knows I'm out with you, so something must be wrong." She hustled to her phone and swiped her screen on the last ring. "Yeah, Carla. What's up?"

"Sorry to bother you, boss, but I just wanted you to know that one of the Canadian guests took a tumble on the paddleboard while Jo was giving her a lesson, and she hit her head on the way down. Doc put some suture strips on her cut and said she should be fine, but I just thought you'd want to know."

"Okay, I'm heading in. Thanks, Carla, we'll be there in about twenty minutes."

"I'll meet you on the dock and fill you in." Carla ended the call.

"Everything okay?" Allie asked with concern in her voice.

"One of the guests fell and cut her head while Jo was giving her a paddleboard lesson. We'll need to head in so I can talk to Doc about what happened and file an incident report."

"Is she okay?"

"Carla said she'll be fine."

"I bet that was Linda. I know she had another private lesson with Jo today."

"Carla didn't distinguish which Canadian guest."

"It was Linda."

"Well…" Kate kissed the word down Allie's neck. "I'm sorry to cut this trip a little short, but—"

"No need to apologize." Allie moaned as she tilted her head back. "The morning was perfect. And if you keep doing that, we'll never make it back to shore anytime soon."

With a groan and a heavy sigh, Kate agreed. "Yeah, we really do need to get going. How about a rain check and a bribe?"

"A bribe?"

"Would you like to steer her in?"

"What, are you kidding? Um, yes." She smiled. "Best bribe ever."

As they walked out of the bedroom, instead of following Kate up the steps to the helm, Allie raised a finger and motioned to give her a minute. Kate nodded and watched her walk to the side of the boat, bow her head in the direction of her father's urn, and blow a kiss.

"Okay, now I'm ready." She turned and scampered over to Kate and up the steps.

Because of the urgency regarding an injured guest, Kate had Allie kick up the knots on their way back. She texted Carla, and as they entered the lagoon, she took the helm. Allowing Allie to operate her baby in open sea was one thing, but docking her was a trust she was not quite ready to give.

"How's our guest?" Kate called as she powered off the yacht and tossed Carla the mooring line.

"She's fine." Carla quickly secured the line to the dock cleat, extended a hand, and helped them off the boat.

"Thanks, Carla," Allie said. "Did you get a chance to look at my boat?"

"I did, and you are good to go."

"Really? What was wrong with it?"

"Just a little wiring situation that was easily fixed."

"Carla, you're a godsend. I'll text Olivia and let her know."

"Well, I have been known to fix a few things around here from time to time." Carla raised a brow toward Kate. "Now." She turned back to Allie. "How was your time at sea?"

"It was…" she said as she shrugged her backpack on and glanced at Kate. "Better than expected."

"I bet," Carla smirked.

Kate faced Allie. "I need to go talk to Doc. How about an early dinner at my place? I thought we could, you know." She leaned in and kissed her. "Maybe do a little more stargazing and cash in that rain check."

"You're on. What time should I be there?"

"How about five o'clock? That should give me enough time to get a handle on what happened and check on the guest."

"Five it is."

They kissed once more before Allie headed down the dock toward the casitas.

"Did I just see what I thought I just saw?"

Kate felt the heat of embarrassment flush her cheeks. "Stop, it's nothing."

"The fuck it is. Come here." Carla grabbed Kate and wrapped her in a tight hug. "Boss, I'm so happy for you."

Kate squirmed. "Well, thank you, but there's still a part of me that feels like I'm cheating on Brooke."

"You're not cheating on her. It's what she would want, and it's what you would want for her if things were reversed."

True. If the tables were turned, she would want Brooke to move on and find someone else to make her happy. Still, it was so much easier said than done. "Anyway." She waved a dismissive hand. "Fill me in on what happened."

"Well, apparently, Jo and the Canadian guest, Linda, have hooked up. Jo was giving her a private paddleboard lesson. At one point, Linda apparently leaned over to kiss her, lost her balance, and fell. She hit her head on the tip of Jo's paddle on her way down. She's more embarrassed than hurt."

Kate shook her head. "What am I going to do with Jo?"

"Nothing. They're together consensually, and this was an accident."

"Well, I still need to talk to Doc and make sure everything's okay. Now then, about—"

"Gizmo!" Mila's shaky voice made them turn as Gizzy ran past. "That damn pig," Mila called as she limped up to them.

"What'd she take this time?" Kate sighed.

"Carrots. I guess the cake tonight will be a few shy of its main ingredient."

"I'm sure there're more carrots, Mila." Kate placed an arm on her shoulder.

"Don't you go cozying up to me." She huffed as she stepped away. "After what you did. You're no better than the pig."

"What'd I do?" Kate chuckled.

"Don't *what'd I do* to me. I saw you raiding the kitchen before you went sneaking off this morning without even asking me to fix you some breakfast." Mila said the words as though they were laced in hurt and disgust.

"I didn't want to burden you so early in the morning."

"And what in hell's name do you think I was doing? Sleeping in? I have a resort of hungry ladies to feed. And did you even eat what you stole, 'cause I sure as hell know you can't cook worth a damn."

"Mila." Kate opened her arms to give her a hug. "You know no one can hold a candle to your cooking skills."

Mila playfully slapped at Kate's arms. "Oh no, you don't, Kate Williams. You might own this resort, but that don't mean I won't take a wooden spoon to you."

Carla chuckled, clearly enjoying watching the entertainment from the sidelines.

"And don't you be taking her side." Mila wagged a finger at Carla. "You two are in cahoots and up to no good. I can feel it in my bones. I may be old, but I ain't no fool, and I ain't blind or deaf."

Carla held up her hands in surrender.

Mila grunted as she looked at them with stern eyes, spat at the ground, and turned. "Don't go stealing no more food. If you need something, just say so. At least when the pig steals food, she has the courtesy to take only one thing," she grumbled as she hobbled away.

"Let me go calm her down," Carla called over her shoulder as she approached Mila.

Kate watched Mila slap Carla's arm a few times before they settled into a slow gait toward the kitchen. They were her rock on this island: Mila the mother figure she never had, and Carla doubled as her best friend and the sister she had always wanted. "Come on, Giz." Kate patted her thigh as she turned and headed toward her house. Gizmo trotted by her side, carrot juice dripping from her chin. "Looks like we both need to brush up on our stealing skills." She took a moment and glanced over her shoulder at her yacht as a flash of heat washed over her.

"I know that look." Brooke pointed a playful finger in Kate's face as she walked backward in front of her. "You're happy," she said as she turned and positioned herself next to her.

"I am." Kate nodded. "But I'm also conflicted."

"Why? She seems wonderful."

"She is, but she's not you."

"Don't do that."

"Do what?"

"Don't compare us. It's not fair to put that on her. You have to let her be her own person to you, Kate. She deserves that, and you deserve to share the next chapter of your life with someone special."

"I'm doing fine." Kate brushed off her thoughts.

"No, babe, you're not. You're stuck. Just like you were when I first met you. You were scared to get clean and sober because life was so much easier when you didn't have to deal with your feelings. To just stay in a state of numbness."

"Stop." Kate turned to Brooke. "It's not the same."

"Yes, it is. You grew the moment you finally allowed yourself to feel vulnerable. To trust that I wasn't going to hurt or abandon you."

"But you did abandon me. You died," Kate spat.

"And you didn't," Brooke snapped back. "Don't use my death as an excuse to numb out again. Allow yourself to be happy once more and embrace the feeling."

"You know you're beginning to sound more and more like Carla?"

"Well, maybe that's because she's right."

"Now you definitely sound like her. Please don't tell me I now have two voices stuck in my head."

Brooke shrugged, then broke into a run. "Last one to the house pops the popcorn."

"Hey, no fair," Kate called as she sprinted up the path and stumbled when Gizmo knocked into her as she ran past. "Oh, you too, huh?"

When she reached the patio, she looked around for Brooke but saw only Gizmo lying on the one lounge chair and snorting as though she was announcing her win. "Okay, all right, I'll pop you a small bowl of popcorn," she said through heavy breaths as she entered her kitchen, retrieved the hot air popper and poured a spoonful of kernels in. She leaned against the kitchen counter as she waited for the bowl to fill, and thought about Allie. The voice in her head was right: Allie deserved to be seen as who she was, not as a comparison to Brooke. Kate had spent the past five years wrapping herself in an emotional numbness. It was time to feel again.

CHAPTER TEN

"Hey, Reba." Allie hit the speaker icon as she stood frowning in front of the mirror, trying to decide if she should tuck in or leave out the tail of the sheer linen dress shirt.

"Don't hey, Reba me. You were supposed to text me this morning after you buried your dad so I knew you were okay, and there's been nothing but radio silence from you."

"Sorry, after burying dad, I kinda got a little emotional, and Kate suggested we soak in her Jacuzzi to take the edge off. We kinda—"

"She has a Jacuzzi? On her yacht?"

"She does, and tonight I'm going to her house for dinner."

"Damn, girl."

"I know, right? In fact, I'm getting dressed right now, and I can't decide if I should tuck my shirt in or leave it out."

"Leave it out, it's easier access."

"Reba," she scolded as she untucked her shirt.

"Oh, come on. First yachting, then dinner. Tell me you don't think that's a prelude to sex."

"That ship already sailed, and it was amazing." She quickly leveled down the volume before Reba's scream shattered her speaker, then giggled as she shared the exciting news.

"Okay, I'm totally jealous, as in, oozing. Congratulations, Allie, I knew you would get laid while you were there."

"Well, like I said before, that was never my intention, but thank you."

"I know, but seriously…ocean, sun, bikinis, booze, and babes? I'd dip my ladle in that soup mix any day."

"Okay, first of all, I don't even want to unpack that statement, and secondly, when we made love, it just kinda happened organically. It was beautiful."

"Aww, that's so sweet. I'm totally happy for you."

"Well, don't read into it too much. There're a lot of obvious hurdles in the way. She lives here, I have to get back to Mom and the restaurant, and oh, not to mention, she's rich, and I'm not."

"What does that have to do with anything?"

"Seriously? Tell me something, Reba, how many times in our lives were we ever invited to hang with the rich kids we knew? To go to any of their functions, parties, or even have one ask us out?"

Silence.

"Exactly. And not to mention, I'd have to save for months just to take Kate out on the type of date she's accustomed to."

"Maybe she doesn't care about things like that."

"She's a trust-fund baby to a billionaire enterprise, her yacht has twice as many amenities as my parents' house and my apartment combined, and she owns an island. Of course she cares about stuff like that. If she didn't, she wouldn't be living like this. No, Kate Williams is out of my league, and we both know it. But I still have a few more days on the island, so we'll see how it all plays out. If nothing else…" It was the beginning of a statement she dreaded saying out loud. "At least I'll have one hell of a memory to bring home." Even if deep down, she wanted so much more. "Hey, I need to get going," she said as her eye caught the time. "Sorry about not texting earlier."

"You can make it up to me when you get home. A lunch with all the details goes a long way toward forgiveness."

"Thanks, Reba. I'll call you tomorrow and let you know how it goes."

"Hell, we both know how it's going to go. I'll be thinking about you tonight while I babysit Melissa and watch repetitive kids shows until I want to stick a fork in my eye. No wonder my sister acquired a taste for vodka."

Allie chuckled. "Go be the amazing auntie that you are. I'll call you tomorrow."

She disconnected the line, did a final check in the mirror, and headed out the door. She was an hour early but wanted to stop by the shack down by the pier, grab a glass of wine, and unwind. A few sips would take the edge off the lack of self-confidence that was starting to creep in. Not so much about her abilities in the bedroom; it was more about her economic insecurities. But maybe Reba was right, maybe Kate didn't care as much about the gap between them as she did. After all, she wasn't getting that vibe from Kate. In fact, just the opposite. Maybe Allie's self-induced paranoia around it reflected her own intimidation getting the better of her. She had heard the "us" and "them" mantra her whole life from her father. No wonder she'd never thought she was good enough.

Allie sighed as she waved off the thoughts. Besides, did any of it even matter? Having sex with someone didn't automatically mean starting a relationship with them. She rolled her eyes. "God Allie, get out of your head and just enjoy the evening and what's left of your vacation," she said as she rounded the corner of her casita and saw Jo and Linda heading to the beach, hand in hand.

"Linda," Allie called as she jogged over to them. "I heard you got injured. Are you okay?"

Linda lifted a section of her hair and showed off the two suture strips. "It's nothing, really. No more than a nasty scratch."

"Still, that had to hurt."

"It hurt my ego more than anything, and now I have to endure the ruthless teasing from my friends. But..." She playfully nudged Jo's shoulder. "I'll manage, huh, babe?"

Jo leaned in and gave Linda a deep kiss. After a moment or two of uncomfortable awkwardness, Allie cleared her throat. "Well, if you need anything, just let me know."

"Oh, I'm taking good care of her, don't you worry." Jo winked.

I bet you are, Allie thought under her smile. "Well, then, I guess I'll leave you two lovebirds alone. It's nice to see you. Both of you." And that statement was true. Each of them had taken the time to make her feel welcome when she'd arrived. Why wouldn't she want the best for both?

"Thanks, Allie from LA. We'll talk more at dinner, eh?"

"Oh, um, actually, I won't be at the table this evening. I have other dinner plans," she bashfully replied as she flicked her eyes toward Kate's house.

Linda and Jo gave each other a knowing glance. "Well," Linda said, "in that case, you and I have a lunch date tomorrow to compare notes over a drink."

Allie pointed a playful finger at her. "That's a date. You guys have a nice night and stay away from paddleboards." Allie continued down the walkway, humming more from happiness than a tune stuck in her head when she heard glass shatter. She backtracked to the kitchen where Mila stood leaning against a commercial-grade stainless steel sink, rubbing her hands. Glass pieces littered the floor, surrounded by a pool of brown liquid.

"Mila?" She stepped inside, and Mila instantly turned her back to her.

"Get out. No one's allowed in here. Go on, get. Supper's not ready yet," she said over her shoulder as she glared.

Allie took another step closer. "I was just passing by and I—"

"Girl, you deaf or something? I said, go on, get."

"I heard you, but it looks to me like there's a mess that needs to be cleaned up, so why don't I help you with that, okay?" Allie grabbed a small trash can, bent, and carefully pinched the larger glass pieces and disposed of them.

"Stop. I said, get out. Besides, you'll cut yourself, and that'll be another mess I'll have to clean up."

"I've been cleaning up broken jars and glasses since I was a kid. My family owns a restaurant in LA, so I know what I'm doing."

Mila snarled. "You don't know nothing."

"Well, I have been accused of that too. Won't you please just let me help you?"

Mila huffed her surrender as she held on to the countertop and used it for assistance as she stood. Within minutes, Allie had swept and wiped down the floor.

"Now then." She grabbed a smock off a hook and wrapped it around her waist. "What else can I help you with? I know my way around a commercial kitchen."

"You can get your ass on outta here. I don't need no help."

"Well, how about this. I won't help you. I'll just stand over here and keep an eye out for Gizmo in case she decides to steal something."

Mila grunted. "Just stay out of my way. And don't be taking nothing. You're worse than that old pig," she said as she began mixing and kneading contents in a bowl.

Allie leaned against the wall and placed her hands in the two large front pockets of the smock. She could tell Mila was struggling but opted to respect her words and not step in. It was enough for her to just watch the master at work in her kitchen. But when Mila grabbed a spice jar and struggled to open it, she approached, gently wrapped her fingers around Mila's bony hand and spoke softly to her. "These things are just impossible to open at times," she said as she twisted the lid off the mason jar marked, oregano.

"Just a pinch," Mila grunted as she rubbed her hands and eyed Allie with suspicion. "And those two." Mila nodded toward a couple canisters full of dried herbs. Allie reached over and grabbed them as the next grunt of directions came. "And a quarter cup of that." Mila pointed to an unmarked jar that upon opening, hinted of cinnamon.

Allie did as she was told but still didn't notice anything unique about the combination of spices that would give the food that pop-in-the-mouth flavor she had come to associate with Mila's cooking. "Anything else?"

Mila was quiet, then bent and struggled to retrieve a large jar from under the table. "You need to add four tablespoons of this, or it ain't gonna taste the way it should."

Allie twisted open the container, took a sniff, and her senses came alive. "I smell ginger, cloves, nutmeg and...ow, ow..." Allie put the jar down and rubbed her shoulder where Mila was smacking her with a wooden spoon.

"Did I tell you to sniff it? Huh? What's wrong with you? Gimme that." Mila snatched back the container. "Don't you be sticking your nose where it ain't welcome."

Allie smiled as she took a step back. "Sorry. It's just that, your food is so amazing, I was just curious what your secret was to make it taste so flavorful."

"And if you think I'm going to tell you, you got something wrong with your head. Now go on, you're wearing on my nerves, so get."

Not to be deterred, Allie leaned against the sink and folded her arms. "You know, ever since I was a kid, I've worked in my parents' restaurant. My whole life, I've played around with different combinations of spices, hoping to make what we serve more flavorful, and I've never been able to even come close to the amazing combinations you have created. You are very gifted, Mila. A true artist when it comes to cooking."

Mila huffed, but Allie could have sworn the corners of her mouth twitched up ever so slightly before returning to their typical stern expression. Mila turned her back, splashed a palmful of flour over a ball of dough and began stretching and pulling at the paste. After a moment, she craned her neck. "You still here? I thought I told you to get."

"Okay, okay." Allie took off the apron and placed it back on the hook. "I'm going."

"Good. And on your way out, grab those plates over there, and then check to see if the water's boiling."

Allie smiled and did as she was told. When the salad was finally tossed, lasagna made, plantains fried, and sauces poured, Mila notified Jo that the food was ready to take to the guests.

"Who's this for?" A tray with two full plates of food was set off to the side.

"That's for Kate. Don't suppose you'd know anything about it?"

Allie smiled.

"Uh-huh. Well, normally, Carla takes Kate's food up to the house, but she seems to be running a little late."

"I can do it. In fact, that's exactly where I need to be right now."

"Uh-huh." Mila grunted again, then cocked her head toward the food. "Well, go on, get. And use the golf cart parked out back."

"Thanks, Mila, and thank you for—"

"I don't have time for chitchat. I got my hands full here. Now you going to take that up to Kate, or do I have to do it myself?"

"I'm going. I'm going." Allie grabbed the tray, placed it in the cart, and followed the path until it circled in front of Kate's house. She parked next to another golf cart, retrieved the tray, and just as she was about to knock, she heard Kate and Carla's voices coming from the back patio. A butterfly took flight as she remembered last night's stargazing and wondered if that same after-dinner entertainment would be the prelude to other more enjoyable things to gaze upon. She began humming again, and right before she rounded the corner and announced her presence, she heard Carla say something that froze her in her tracks.

"Yes, boss, stop worrying. She's back to working order. I made sure that when I removed the battery cable, it would be easy to reverse."

"Thanks, Carla. I just feel so bad that I had you do it in the first place."

"Well…maybe next time, you might want to hold off on sabotaging a guest's boat until you get the whole story."

The punch to Allie's gut felt like the wind had been knocked out of her. She stumbled backward and had to lean against the wall for support. She gulped at the air to catch her breath and calm her heart rate as a moment of dizziness took hold. There must have been a mistake to what she'd just heard. Surely, she'd taken it out of context. Kate would not have done that to her. No, she shook her. No, no, no, no, no. She refused to believe the woman she was falling for would do such a thing.

"Please tell me I'm not hearing what I think I'm hearing." Allie rounded the corner, her disbelief now teetering on anger.

Kate and Carla jumped. "Oh shit," Carla mumbled.

"Yeah, oh shit," Allie snapped as she placed the tray on the lounge chair and squared off with Kate. "You're the reason my boat wouldn't start? You not only knew about this, you ordered it?"

"Gotta go." Carla pushed past Allie as she scurried off.

Kate approached with extended arms. "I can explain."

Allie jerked away. "First, you need to look me in the eyes and tell me you did not intentionally sabotage my boat." She stared Kate down. "Please, Kate. Tell me you didn't do it."

Kate averted her eyes.

And there it was, a confession by omission. The reality of it was so incomprehensible, it froze her mentally and physically. Like when she'd stood in the doorway staring at Shelly making love to another woman because she just couldn't, no, wouldn't, believe what was happening. "Why?" she said as tears welled in her eyes. "Why?" She repeated through a breath that felt like a hundred-pound weight was pressing against her chest as she searched Kate's eyes for some redemption.

"I thought you were a treasure hunter."

Allie advanced into Kate's personal space. "I told you I wasn't."

"But you had a metal detector, and I had to be sure." Kate's eyes were pleading.

"No, what you had to do was believe me when I told you the truth."

Kate backed away and began to pace. "Allie, you have to understand where I was coming from. What I've been through my entire life. What people have done—"

"No, Kate. This isn't about you. I needed to bury my father out there." She waved to the ocean. "It was his dying wish,

Kate. His dying wish. And the anxiety I've had thinking there was a chance that I'd brought him all this way and might not be able to do that was gut-wrenching. How dare you put that on me?"

"But I didn't know about your dad's dying wish when I told Carla to do what she did." Kate took a step toward her.

"Well, when you found out, you didn't even have the decency to tell me the truth." Allie paused as she tilted her head in thought. "Wait a minute. I told you about my father last night. You could have had Carla fix it then. Instead, you had me go out with you this morning, and even after we made love, you still had me believe there was something mechanically wrong with that boat. Wow." She shook her head as she backed away from Kate as though distancing herself from the person inflicting her pain would make it hurt any less.

"I was…embarrassed." Kate lowered her head.

"Well, maybe next time, you'll trade your embarrassment for integrity."

"I'm sorry," Kate said in a soft apologetic tone as she hunched her shoulders and lowered her head.

"Yeah, well, so am I." Allie tuned and scurried to the cart as Kate called after her. She hopped in and slammed her foot against the accelerator as tears streamed down her cheeks. Frustrated that the cart wasn't going as fast as she wanted, she started stomping on the peddle and rocked herself back and forth. "A child could outwalk this." She scowled at the cart for its inability to instantly transport her away from Kate.

After what seemed like the longest distance she had ever traveled, she pulled up outside the kitchen and parked. Her heart was pounding against her chest, and she was choking on every breath she inhaled. She bent forward and rested her head on her hands that were still white-knuckling the steering wheel. She took a moment to let her emotions rush to the surface. "Fuck this, and fuck Kate." She spat the words through tear-soaked lips. "I should have known." She huffed as she threw her body against the seat cushion. Anything that was too good to be true...was. Period. She was probably just some hookup to Kate. She exhaled a breath and shook her head. What a fool she was for entertaining the slightest thought that her emerging feelings for Kate could possibly be mutual.

She hopped out of the golf cart and kicked a tire in a last burst of anger, then again for good measure. Stupid slow-moving vehicle. Seriously, in this day and age, they couldn't get these things to move any faster? She grumbled her frustration at the cart, Kate, and the world as she stomped back to her casita.

She threw herself on the bed, had one more gut-wrenching cry, then grabbed her suitcase and flung it on the mattress. She scurried around the room, reacting on raw emotions as she grabbed and gathered clothes and toiletries and threw them in one big pile into the suitcase. She slammed the hard-shell case shut but snarled when it wouldn't close. In an attempt to defy the laws of physics and get the sides to touch enough to zip the edges, she sat on the case. But it still wouldn't close.

She slid off the luggage and down the side of the bed until she came to a stop with a thud on the floor. She brought her legs to her chest, bowed her head in her hands, and took a few meditative breaths. She wished she had never come to this island or had met Kate. No, that wasn't totally true. Up until a few minutes ago, she had never felt so alive. If nothing else, Kate had introduced her to a depth of feelings she had never known. A few more tears leaked out from the corner of her eyes, even though she was trying hard to hold them, and her feelings, back.

"Okay," she whispered as she peeled herself off the floor. "Get it together, Allie." She came here for one reason and one reason only. And now that it was done, there was really no other reason to stay. She wiped her cheeks, rearranged her clothes enough to zip up the edges of the suitcase, and with blind hurt guiding her decision, she shrugged her backpack over her shoulders, extended the handle of her suitcase, and walked out of Casita Four for the last time.

She scurried to the dock. She didn't want to see anyone, especially Kate, for fear of being talked out of her decision. She just wanted to vanish into the night and put this whole thing behind her. When she made it to her boat without incident, she exhaled a sigh of relief. She flung her bags in without concern for dings or dents, and as she bent over to untie the lines, she heard the distinct sound of a golf cart approaching. Damn it. She wasn't in the mood to listen to any more of Kate's justifications.

"Thought you might need some food for your journey."

Allie couldn't help but smile, if only a little, as she turned and faced Mila sitting in her cart, outstretched hand clutching a bag.

"Oh, I'm just…" Allie stood and fumbled for words. "I'm just taking the boat out for an evening dive."

Mila glanced into the boat, and Allie knew by her line of sight that she was looking at her luggage. "Mm-hmm," she murmured as she jiggled the bag.

Allie sighed, approached the cart, and took the offer. "Thank you." The gesture was kind. But the knot in her stomach squelched any pings she had of hunger.

They stood for a moment, gazing at the other. Allie felt the urge to lean in and give Mila a good-bye hug. As crotchety as the old woman was, there was something about her that tugged at Allie's heart. But not only that, Mila was truly a master at the art of cooking, and that alone earned Allie's respect. She began to bend with outstretched arms, when Mila shooed her away. "Now move back. Go on, get. I got things to do, and you're standing in my way."

Allie stepped back as Mila began a sloppy three-point turn and headed back to the resort but stopped the cart and called over her shoulder, "She might not have the best judgment at times, but her heart is pure."

"I'm sorry, who are you talking about?" Allie called back.

Mila huffed as she twisted around, locked eyes with Allie, and grunted. "Who do you think?"

And with those words still lingering in the air, Mila drove away and vanished into the darkness.

A moment of doubt flashed through Allie as she glanced at the hill and focused on the house as tears welled, and she thought about the evening that could have been and the woman who probably had no idea how much she'd touched Allie's heart. Oh well, she thought as she hopped in the boat, they'd shared a moment in time in a fantasy world that looked nothing like her reality. It was now time to retreat back to a place and space that might not resemble what she wanted out of life, but it was *her* life, and it was familiar and predictable.

She fired up the boat and was relieved to hear the engine turn over. She shook her head again at the thought of Kate sabotaging it, and with renewed disgust, she activated the Chartplotter computer and headed out to sea and to the life she called home.

❖

"Sorry a family emergency is bringing you back so soon, but I'm sure glad to see you were able to get her fixed," Olivia said as she grabbed the lines Allie threw out and moored the boat. "Like I said, I won't charge you for the rental."

"Charge me. Seems the reason your boat wouldn't start was on my end, not yours." She handed her luggage to Olivia. "Want me to grab the gear?"

Olivia waved her off. "Nah, I'll lock up the container and deal with that in the morning. Phil's already loaded and waiting for you. We gotta get going."

Allie had called ahead and let Olivia know she was returning early and asked if she could give her any suggestions on the quickest way to get from Nassau to Miami, expecting that she would have to stay the night at a hotel and deal with the usual transportation modes in the morning. She was pleasantly pleased when Olivia had told her she knew a guy who flew a little two-seater over to Miami every night loaded with bags of mail and packages. For cash under the table, he was known to make room for a passenger. He could get her there by eleven, just in time for a red-eye back to LA, which she'd booked for a change fee that was almost as expensive as the original ticket. It was probably a reckless financial decision to make, but it was one she would worry about later.

"Thanks, Olivia. The boat and the gear worked perfectly." She threw her luggage into the back of Olivia's Jeep, and hopped in.

"Told ya. She's not much to look at, but she's got guts." Olivia fired up her Jeep and threw it in drive.

"She sure does, more guts than most people I know," Allie said with a bite as she thought about Kate.

Olivia sped to a small airport, which consisted of a tin shed and a stretch of concrete that had weeds growing through countless cracks. She swallowed a lump of anxiety that would have normally caused her to rethink her decision, but her anger and exhaustion were numbing her fear of flying. At this stage, she just wanted to get home.

She hugged Olivia good-bye, and they promised to stay in touch as Phil called out that they needed to get going. He was already behind schedule. She hurried to the plane and nestled in between two overstuffed canvas bags as he shoved her luggage in the back. She buckled up, and as the plane lifted off into the darkness, she rested her forehead against the window and exhaled a heavy breath. Through the blinking of the plane's strobe lights, she watched the hypnotic twinkling of Nassau fade away, and with it, all of her hopes for what could have been.

If only.

CHAPTER ELEVEN

K nock, knock."
    Kate heard Carla's distant voice in the fog of her sleepy mind as she blinked herself awake. She tried to focus on a blurry image approaching with an object in hand and depositing it on the table by her lounge chair.

"You into a new style of eating, or is that Gizmo's artwork?"

Kate tilted her head and glanced at morsels, crumbs, and food smears on and around the table and deck, remnants from last night's untouched dinner.

"Giz ate it." She flopped her arm in the direction of Gizmo, who was stretched out on the chair beside her. "I'll clean it up later." Her energy level was as bottomed out as her hunger. Did Carla actually think she was motivated enough to perform a task right now? Pfft. Yeah, that wasn't going to happen anytime soon.

"So you're telling me"—Carla bent, swapped out the plates, and hovered over Kate—"you didn't eat a single bite of your dinner again."

"I'm just not hungry." Kate yawned and scrubbed a hand over her face.

Carla crossed her arms. "It's been three weeks, boss. The hunger strike thing is getting old."

Kate folded her arms on top of her head and groaned. "I shouldn't have done what I did to Allie. Why didn't you stop me from making such a bad decision?"

"Oh, so now it's my fault?" Carla huffed. "I see."

"I fucked up."

"Yep, you did," Carla said as she sat on a tiny sliver of chair not taken up by Gizmo's sprawling body, grabbed a slice of papaya, and took a bite. "So what's preventing you from flying to LA, waltzing into her café, and apologizing?"

"I texted her, left messages, and I sent a telescope with a card saying I was sorry. Since she hasn't replied to any of those, I doubt I'd be welcome in her restaurant."

"A telescope?" Carla snorted. "Instead of dozens of roses? Boss, you need to brush up on your how-to-get-the-girl-back skills."

"You don't understand, she likes to star…never mind." She waved a dismissive hand.

"Look, all I'm saying is, if you want her back, you need to get your sorry little ass on a plane and go to her."

That was just it; she had never had to chase anything or anyone before. If she wanted something, she'd bought it. If she'd desired a woman, no problem, she'd had her pick. And when her little romantic flings had ended, no big deal because none of them had fulfilled her. But to be fair, nothing in her life at that time had. But that had all stopped when Brooke had come along. For the first time in Kate's life, she'd not only felt content, but she'd actually worried about someone leaving her. A thought that had never occurred to her before but seemed to be playing out for the second time in her life.

"No," she said. "I'm not going to do that."

"Why? You think you're above groveling?"

"No, it's just that, um…" She glanced at Carla with a hint of embarrassment. "I've never had to do it before."

Carla threw her head back in laughter. "You mean to say, you've never had to grovel? In your life?"

Kate lowered her gaze and shook her head. "Having to grovel or apologize was never something a Bennett did. That's what Dad's lawyers and associates were paid to do."

"Wow," Carla said. "That's kinda crazy, boss. Everyone's had to grovel from time to time. It's like a rite of passage. In fact, I don't know anyone who's had a successful relationship without mastering it."

"Carla," Kate said in a sappy high-pitched voice as she glanced at her.

"Oh no. I know that look, and the answer is definitely no."

"You don't even know what I'm about to ask you."

"Doesn't matter. I can already tell I won't like it."

"What would you say if I paid you to fly to LA and grovel for me?"

"Oh no, baby doll, this hole is yours to crawl out of."

"Please?"

"Nope."

"Fine." Kate scoffed as she pushed herself deeper in the cushion. "Then you're fired."

"Uh-huh." Carla's phone dinged, she stood, returned the text, and without looking up, continued. "And who the hell do you think's gonna run this place while you're up here feeling sorry for yourself?"

Kate let out an exhausted sigh. "I'm tired, and my heart hurts...again."

Carla started to walk away. "Yeah, well, I can't help you there. I'm fired, remember?"

"Where are you going?" Kate said through a long desperate sigh. "Come back here."

Carla turned. "Oh, am I hired again? Well, in that case, let's talk about my new signing bonus."

Even with the heavy layer of pain from the mental flogging she had inflicted on herself these past few weeks, Kate managed to smile at that comment. Good 'ol Carla. She stood and hugged her. "You know I wouldn't know what to do with my life without you."

"Uh-huh. Just remember that before your mouth goes one direction and your brain goes another. Now, eat something, or I'll let Mila know you're feeding her food to Gizmo. She'll get on you with that spoon of hers."

"You wouldn't dare."

Carla raised her brow. "Wouldn't I?"

They stared at each other, neither backing down until Kate picked up a slice of watermelon, bit the tip off, and chewed. "Happy now?"

"Well, aren't you the petulant little child?" Carla chuckled as her phone dinged again. "I gotta get going. I have a resort to run," she said as she gave Kate's shoulder a loving squeeze. "Look, just fly to LA, apologize over and over, emphasize how sorry you are for being an ass, then shower her with a shitload of flowers until you wear her down, and she gives you a second chance."

"And if she doesn't?"

"Then at least you tried. But I saw the look in her eyes the day you two stepped off your yacht, and I could tell she was really into you."

Kate cringed as the pain of those words hit her gut. "I know," was all she could say as she glanced at Carla. And maybe *that* was the root of the problem. The two of them had connected. She'd felt the pull from the moment she'd met Allie, and she'd wanted to embrace that feeling as much as resist it.

"With Brooke," she said more to herself than Carla, "it was easy. She seemed to accept all the times I was being an ass."

"Allie isn't Brooke. And maybe it's about time you grew into a new pair of shoes. If Allie calls you out in a way that makes you uncomfortable, then I say good for her. 'Bout time someone put a Bennett in their place." Carla lightheartedly chuckled as she began walking away. "Now, go to her. Sometimes, all the money in the world can't fix what a simple gesture of sincerity can."

"But…"

"Nope." Carla called as she rounded the corner. "That's all I got. Eat your breakfast before I tell on you."

Kate stood frozen for a moment, not knowing what to say or do until the sound of Gizmo repositioning herself on her chair refocused her attention. She strolled back over, sat next to her, grabbed another wedge of watermelon, took a bite, and gave the rest to Giz. She repeated this until the plate was empty. One bite for her, the rest for Gizmo. "There, breakfast eaten." She scrubbed her fingers under Gizzy's chin, stretched, and slowly peeled herself off the chair. "I think I'll go snorkeling for a while, sweetie. I need to clear my mind. See you in a bit."

She grabbed her gear, jogged down to the ocean, and took a moment to glance toward the area of the beach where she and Allie had shared an evening. Her stomach tightened as Allie's smiling face flashed in her mind. "Great," she grumbled. "Now I'm going to have the image of you stuck in my head too."

She put on her gear, dove into an incoming wave, and headed for the reef and the area where she knew Bruce liked to hang out. Sure enough, within minutes, he approached. She stopped swimming, pushed up her mask, and treaded water as he circled her.

"He's finally come around," Brooke said as she appeared next to her.

"Yeah, he has." Kate reached out, letting her fingers trickle over his skin. "I think he's lonely, and I worry about him when he doesn't join me."

"Well, I'm starting to worry about *you*."

Kate glanced over. "I'm fine."

"No, you're not. You're as lonely as Bruce."

"I'm fine," Kate repeated in a louder voice and slapped the water. Bruce flicked his tail and quickly swam away, obviously startled by the outburst. "Shit. Sorry, Bruce," she called after him. "Now look what you did." She glanced at Brooke.

"Me? I'm nothing more than a figment of your imagination," Brooke said as she backstroked around Kate.

Kate exhaled as her eyes began to well with tears that were filled with heartache. She wasn't sure if they were for Brooke or Allie. "You know I miss you," she said.

"I miss you too. Now, go to her, and stop being an ass. In the short time you've spent with her, your heart came alive again. *You* came alive again."

"What if she won't take me back?" She bounced the conversation she had with Carla to Brooke, obviously replaying the words in her mind.

"You'll never know until you ask." Brooke swam to Kate and cupped her face. "If you want her, you'll need to go after her. No one's going to rescue you from yourself on this one."

"And if she says no?"

"She won't."

"You don't know that."

"No, I don't. But don't you think it's worth the risk to find out?"

She knew in her heart that was what she needed to do, but that didn't mean she wasn't uncomfortable with the thought of doing it. And therein lay her other dilemma. It had been over ten years since she was last back in the City of Angels, and she dreaded the thought of returning, if only for a bit. It was a place that represented a life she never wanted to return to and demons that still called to her. If only Allie would reply to her messages, she could fly her out here so they could talk. Did she really have to physically go to LA?

"Yes, you have to physically go there," Brooke said.

Kate waved at the thought as though she was shooing a pesky gnat. "When did you get so pushy?"

"The moment you began talking yourself out of something that could be the best thing in your life right now."

"Fine, I'll book a flight," she grumbled. "Happy now?"

Brooke smiled but remained silent as Kate stared at the sparkles in her eyes until they turned into the sun's rays glistening off the water. It was obvious she would be arguing with herself and reliving all the things that she should have done differently until she did what she knew she needed to do. As she pulled her mask down onto her face and inserted the snorkel's mouthpiece, she conceded that maybe it *was* time to stop waiting for others to rescue her.

"Boss, boss?"

She barely heard the words over the sound of the Jet Ski approaching, but the urgency in Carla's voice was undeniable. Something was up, and whatever it was, wasn't good. She pulled her mask and snorkel off in one yank. "Carla, that's wrong?"

"Get on. Mila collapsed in the kitchen. Doc's with her now."

"Mila?" The whisper of her name barely made it through the lump building in her throat. "What happened?"

"Get on, and I'll fill you in."

Kate grabbed Carla's extended arm and used it to help pull herself onto the Ski. "I'm on," she said as soon as she was settled in behind her.

With the flick of her wrist, Carla opened her up full throttle, and over the sound of the Ski and wind, Carla filled her in on the situation. "Jo was walking by the kitchen and heard bowls being knocked around. When she peeked in, she saw Mila on the floor, unconscious. That's when she called me and Doc. MedFlight is on their way, and Doc told me to come get you."

"Is she, um…" Words were hard to form as anxiety gripped her stomach. Not Mila. That stubborn old woman was supposed to live forever. But Kate had seen the signs—hell, everyone had—but like most things in her life that were too hard to accept, she'd chosen to ignore them and hope that the status quo would somehow last forever. "Is she going to be okay?" Kate needed to hear the words that would calm her pounding heart and let her know that the one they all looked to as the mother figure of the resort would still hold that title.

"Don't know yet."

The next few minutes seemed like agony as her mind whisked her back in time and made her relive the most agonizing day of her life and the out-of-control feeling she'd had when Brooke had collapsed, and she was the one making the call to MedFlight. She closed her eyes and willed those awful memories from her mind as she tightened her grip around Carla's waist and nuzzled into her back. The gesture wasn't going to change the outcome of the situation, but for that brief moment, clinging tight to Carla gave her a sense of security and hope.

"Hold on, I'm going to beach her," Carla said as she ran the Ski onto the sand.

Kate hopped off, propelled by fear and adrenaline, and dug her bare feet deep into the soft sand. But she stumbled when she couldn't quite gain traction and broke the fall with outstretched hands. She took a moment to reposition herself, then sprinted to the kitchen with Carla in tow.

Her breath was heavy, and her heart pounded as they entered the kitchen. Jo and most of the staff were standing off to the side, looking nervous and concerned. She focused on Doc hovering over Mila's outstretched body on the floor. Her eyes were closed. The acidic taste of bile scorched the back of Kate's throat as a moment of nausea came on, then quickly subsided when Carla bumped into her shoulder as she pushed past.

"How's she doing, Doc?" Kate said in a whispered voice as she approached, lowered herself on bent knees, and felt a slight tremor release inside her. "Is she…" Kate choked on the words. "Is she—"

"I ain't dead…if that's…what you're asking," Mila said in a weak, barely audible slurred voice in between heavy breaths. "And don't…talk as though…I ain't here."

Kate puffed a breath of relief as she smiled. If the Reaper had come for Mila, she'd probably beaten him off with her wooden spoon. Doc raised her head, locked eyes with her, then motioned toward the other side of the room.

"I'll stay with her," Carla said with reassurance.

Kate nodded and followed Doc over to the corner. "Her left side isn't responsive," Doc said in a low voice as they settled against the wall.

"What does that mean?"

"It means for now, I'm having MedFlight transport her to a Nassau hospital to run some tests."

Kate's stomach lurched. "What kind of tests?"

"I don't want to make an assumption without the facts."

"But if you had to make a guess, what would you say?"

Doc remained quiet.

Kate placed her hand on Doc's forearm and gently squeezed. "Doc, is she going to be okay?"

"If you're asking if she'll live, then, yes, I'm confident she will."

Kate exhaled relief as the weight of the situation eased from her heart. "But?" She could tell the story was only half told.

"But I think she suffered a stroke, the severity of which, I don't know. But let's see what the tests tell us, okay?"

The room began to spin a bit on those words, and the bile Kate had tamped down earlier began to make a repeat appearance. Mila was a proud woman. If it was a stroke, and it limited her ability to do the one and only thing in life she'd identified with, then she would probably wish she had died. It was a thought Kate quickly put out of her mind. Life, even with its challenges, was worth fighting for.

She glanced back at Mila. Carla was holding her hand, and they looked like they were engaged in a conversation when Gizmo came trotting into the kitchen, went right up to Mila, and moved her snout around her cheek, grunting and nuzzling against her. Kate broke away from Doc and hurried over to shoo Gizzy away but stopped when she saw Mila let go of Carla's hand and bring it to Gizmo's snout. "Love...you...too," she whispered.

The growing distinct sound of a helicopter became audible, and within minutes, the medical team had Mila off the floor and strapped into a stretcher. Before they loaded her on the helicopter, Kate grabbed her hand and told her everything would be okay and to not worry about the resort, but of course, her sentiment was met with mumbled words she didn't fully understand but got the gist of. Mila didn't want anyone in her kitchen.

"Well." Carla's hand landed with a thud on her shoulder as they stood on the dock watching the helicopter fade into the distance. "Looks like it's you and me in the kitchen."

"We have a few more hours until lunch. I have an idea." Kate whipped out her cell phone and dialed. She placed an order with a five-star resort in Nassau and arranged for a plane to fly out a fully catered lunch and dinner. This was the last night for this week's round of guests. She and Carla would take them back to Nassau in the morning and spend the afternoon visiting with Mila and getting the update from her doctors. That left one week to find a temporary chef before the next group arrived. She glanced at Gizmo, who stood head tilted to the sky as she sniffed the air.

"She'll be back, girl. I promise." She reached down and scrubbed Gizmo's head. In the meantime, she had several calls to make. Time to put everything and everyone out of her mind as much as possible and focus on what she needed to do.

Chapter Twelve

W hat do you think?" Allie widened her eyes as she anxiously leaned across the table of the booth, waiting for Reba to take a bite of her latest black bean and mushroom burger loaded with all the fixings.

"Oh my God, this is so delicious." Reba moaned as she licked some cashew cheese sauce off her lips.

With a sigh of relief, Allie leaned back and pressed her back against the cushion. "I'm going to call it the Bahama burger." Ever since her return, she had been experimenting with mixing spices to get the same flavors she'd tasted in Mila's cooking. She had yet to perfect it, but she was getting close.

"So." Reba placed the two-handed burger on her plate and scrubbed her fingers with the napkin. "Have you replied to Kate yet?"

Allie shook her head. "No, for the umpteenth time, I still haven't, and I probably won't. Besides, she stopped texting and calling after she sent the telescope." In the days after Allie's return, Kate had inundated her phone with a long list of justifications as to why she'd done what she had. And although Kate sounded sincere, Allie didn't want a laundry list of excuses. She wanted to hear the words, *I miss you*, or, *you mean something to me*. She wanted Kate to stop focusing on the reasons and acknowledge the consequences and hurt it had caused.

But since that never came, she'd buried her grief and disappointment with busying herself at the restaurant and tried to turn her feelings of sadness and anger into her own list of reasons why she should never talk to Kate again. She had really fallen for Kate, even though she'd known deep down that fairy tales never came true, and wishes and dreams were nothing more than a hope and a prayer. And she had a chestful of those, all unanswered.

"You have to admit, that was a pretty awesome *I'm sorry* gift."

Reba's words brought her back to the conversation. "Yeah, I guess." She shrugged.

"Are you fucking kidding me?" Reba said. "That thing has to be worth, what, at least—"

"Twenty thousand dollars." Allie said because she'd googled it after receiving it. Not that she cared, of course. "Keeping it feels like I'm taking a bribe." At first, she'd wanted to send it back but had hesitated when memories of their stargazing night had filled her head, and the feeling of happiness had embraced her heart. Maybe, she'd reasoned as she made room for it in her closet, she'd keep it in the hope that one day, she could actually use it without it feeling bittersweet.

"Okay, first of all, it's not a bribe. You said you sat on her porch and stargazed with her, which I still think is so incredibly romantic. Just call her, Allie. You can't stop thinking about her, and you said the sex was amazing."

"I don't think about her *that* much," she said defensively.

Reba folded her arms, settled back in her seat, and raised an eyebrow.

Allie bent forward, planted her elbows on the table, and buried her face in her hands. "I think I really fell hard for her."

"Ya think?" Reba grabbed the burger and took another bite. "Look," she mumbled as she chewed. "All I'm saying is, so what if she sabotaged your boat? In fact, if you think about it, it's kinda what brought you two together, right? Am I not right?"

"That's not the point. The point is, she thought I lied to her, almost prevented me from burying Dad, and then tried to cover it up. *That's* the point. She should have trusted me in the first place and come clean with me afterward."

"Allie, she's worth like, what, a gazillion dollars? The paparazzi ruthlessly hounded her during her entire life, and I'm sure people were pulling on her right and left. You said she told you her childhood sucked, so maybe trust is the one thing she can't afford to hand out too freely. Besides, she only knew you for, what, a couple of days? Does anyone know anyone in just..." Reba stopped midsentence as her eyes focused on something behind Allie.

"What?"

"Holy shit." Reba nodded toward the doors.

Allie turned, and even though the sun backlit the person who had just stepped into the diner, there was no denying who it was. Board shorts had been replaced with tight jeans, and an equally tight-fitting dress shirt and a designer blazer rounded out the look. Allie let out a gasp as her mind raced as fast as her heart. A swirl of emotions hit her as hurt and excitement collided. "Shit."

What was Kate doing here? Allie took a quick inventory of herself. She knew she probably had flour on her face, food stains on her clothes, and most likely, her hair resembled the makings of a bird's nest. This was not what she'd envisioned reconnecting with Kate to look like. Damn it, this was an ambush. She quickly ducked and sunk so low in her seat, she lost her balance and ended up sliding onto the floor with a thud.

"Oh my God, weirdo, what are you doing?" Reba bent and craned her neck under the table.

"That's her. That's Kate," Allie whispered as she pointed.

"Um, yeah, I know." Reba lifted her head for a moment, then returned. "Wow, she's hotter in person than her photos."

"Reba," Allie barked. "I don't need you to tell me how hot she is. I already know that. Just tell me *where* she is."

"Well, if you would get out from under the table and sit in the seat like a normal person, you would know where she is."

"Just tell me," Allie snapped as she tried to shake off a surge of anxiety. Her heart was still bruised, and depending on the minute of the day, she teetered between wanting to tell Kate off and wanting to profess undying love. She was a walking contradiction, and she knew it. Which was another reason why she hadn't returned any of Kate's calls or texts. She wanted to have control and a better understanding of her emotions when she next spoke to her, and right now, she had neither.

"Okay, okay, hold on." Reba lifted her head again. "She's at the counter talking to your mom. And oh my God."

"What? Oh my God, what?"

"She has the most beautiful bouquet of roses in her hand, and uh oh, busted. Your mom just pointed to us, and she's walking this way."

"Shit," Allie mumbled as she tried to snake herself out from under the table.

"Hi, Allie." Kate approached shyly, raised a questioning brow, and gazed at her. "Is this a bad time?"

"Kate, hi." Allie grunted as she made one final effort and pushed herself up onto the seat. "Wow…um." She patted down her hair and smoothed her clothes as she tried to regain her composure. "What a surprise. What are you doing in LA?"

"I was wondering if maybe I could talk with you."

Reba cleared her throat as she motioned toward Kate with a slight tilt of her head.

"Oh, um, Kate, I'd like to introduce you to my best friend, Reba. Reba, this is Kate Williams."

Reba flicked her hair over her shoulder and extended her hand. "It's a pleasure to meet you. Allie's told me so much about you."

"Really?" Kate returned her gaze to Allie and smiled. "She has, has she?"

Okay, that was enough of the small talk. Now that Kate had forced the hand between them, it was time to take the awkward waltz around the dance floor with her. Just the two of them. Allie twitched her head to the side multiple times until Reba finally got the hint.

"Oh right, yeah, um, I better get going, so you two can um…yeah." Reba slid out of the booth. "It was nice to meet you, Kate."

"Likewise," Kate said as she motioned to the empty seat. "May I?"

Allie nodded, and Kate slid in, extended her hand, and presented Allie with a bouquet of two dozen, long-stemmed white roses. "These are for you."

Allie took them and sniffed. "They're beautiful," she said, and they were. Flowers were one of nature's most magnificent creations. A single bloom could always brighten her day. She laid them on the table and crossed her arms. Time to get serious. "What brings you to LA?"

"Allie." Kate placed her hands on the table, palms up, but when Allie didn't respond to the gesture, she slid them to her side, took a moment to readjust herself in the booth, then held Allie's gaze. Allie had to admit, watching Kate squirm was a bit satisfying. "You…and business."

Allie snorted. Kate would have earned so many forgiveness points toward her cause if she would have just stopped at the "you" part of that sentence.

"Since you haven't replied to any of my messages, I thought it was time to come see you and apologize in person. I'm sorry for what I did. It was wrong. You deserve better. And I was wondering if maybe we could, you know, try again?" Kate's face squished up a bit with trepidation.

A part of Allie had longed to hear those words. Kate was the last thing she thought about before she fell asleep and the first image in her head when she woke. And although a few butterflies were doing an impressive dance around her stomach, there was a part of her that remained reluctant.

"Kate." She still wanted to hear the sentences that would melt the last of her anger away. The words that let her know Kate not only acknowledged what she'd done but acknowledged *her*.

"I know," Kate interrupted. "I ruined it. In fact, to quote Carla, I'm an asshole for what I did. It's just, I grew up watching the people I love lie to gain the upper hand or take advantage of a situation…or someone else. I know that's no excuse for my behavior, but it is something I became accustomed to." Kate averted her eyes. "When I realized you were telling the truth, I should have been honest with you about sabotaging your boat. But I was enjoying our time together so much that I became selfish and wanted you to spend all your time with me. I'm so sorry. I guess I still have a lot to learn…and unlearn." She returned her gaze to Allie. "All I'm asking for is a chance to make it up to you. In fact, how about an all-expenses-paid trip back to the resort? I miss you, Allie, and I'm prepared to grovel if that's what'll take to get a second chance."

Kate was endearing, to say the least, but as Allie sat staring into her pleading eyes, she couldn't shake the fear of a repeat performance. Of how Kate would handle some other misunderstood situation that was bound to come up between them, and how she might always defer to her past as an excuse for her present behavior. "First of all, thank you for apologizing.

Secondly, even if I wanted to take you up on your offer to return to the resort, I can't get away. I have the diner to run."

Allie could tell by her dejected expression that she was digesting the news that she would not, in fact, be taken her up on her proposition. Kate slowly nodded as she glanced around the diner. "How's the restaurant going?"

Allie shrugged as she welcomed the change in conversation. Seemed like they both needed a moment to regroup. "I don't know how much longer we can keep the doors open. Inflation keeps going up, so our suppliers are raising the cost of everything, yet Mom keeps insisting we keep our prices low because our clientele is mostly on a fixed income."

She motioned toward Charlie, who was sitting alone, sipping from the mug of coffee he tightly gripped in his shaky hands. "That's Charlie. He was Dad's military buddy. He comes here every day at eleven o'clock sharp. He sits at the same table, orders the daily special, and has no money to pay for the meal. Dad used to tell him not to worry about it, that he'd just add his meals to a tab that he could pay off later. But Dad never created a tab because he knew Charlie had fallen on hard times ten years ago after his wife died. And since my dad claimed Charlie came to his aid on more than one occasion in the service, he felt like he was paying off a debt *he* owed *him*. And his story is just one of many. Most of our steady clientele is in that same boat. They count on this place for what might be the only meal they can afford in the day."

Kate glanced around the room, and Allie wondered if she could even comprehend what Allie was saying. To grasp what it would have been like to live life without the gift of financial security. To live paycheck to paycheck and have to make a choice between paying rent or putting food on the table.

"That's very kind," Kate said in a low voice as she continued to focus on some of the patrons.

"It's my mom. She keeps the prices low because she feels like she owes it to the community that has kept this place in business all these years, and she won't listen when I tell her we're running out of money. Very soon, no matter how much she wants this place to stay open, reality will dictate otherwise."

"I see. Allie, I can help pay for—"

Allie held up her hand. "No, Kate, don't. You can't buy your way back into my life."

"I didn't mean…I, um, what I meant was…" Kate stumbled, glanced at Allie, and with a nod, dropped the subject. "Okay. So tell me, what's good on the menu? I haven't had lunch yet, and that burger looks pretty good." Kate gestured toward Reba's half-eaten meal left on the table.

"It's a mushroom black bean burger that I was experimenting with, but I didn't make enough of the patty mix for another meal. But." She grinned as she held up her finger. "Today, I made a bunch of vegan shepherd's pies. I'm trying to change the menu and the minds of the customers, one meal at a time. Not like that'll matter if we close down but…" She scooted out of the booth. "Give me a minute, and I'll be right back."

Allie scurried to the kitchen, and the moment she was behind the door, she leaned against the wall, folded forward, and extended her arms to her knees. She took a few gulping breaths and felt as though she was recouping from running a marathon. Anger. Excitement. Confusion. Attraction. All collided inside. If she thought Kate's pull on her body from thousands of miles away had been difficult to resist, sitting across from her at the booth was close to impossible.

"You okay there, Allie?" one of the part-time staff called as she scooped a heaping spoonful of mashed potatoes into a small side bowl.

"Yeah." Allie waved her off. "Just a moment of exhaustion."

The excuse seemed to satisfy the high school kid, who returned to her task at hand. *Get it together, Allie.* She scolded herself as she scurried into the small employee bathroom and grumbled as she checked herself in the mirror. Kate had come into her restaurant looking put together and perfect. She, on the other hand, looked like the walking dead. Bags under her eyes from lack of sleep, no makeup because, yet again, she had been late getting out the door, and a tiny bit of dried sauce in her hair from a mishap and a splash. She leaned into the glass and did her best to freshen up. Still not satisfied but feeling less disheveled, she scurried out of the restroom, grabbed a warm premade casserole dish, took a deep breath, and headed back to Kate and a barrage of memories that were becoming harder and harder to shake off, much less resist.

"Here you go, one shepherd's pie." She scooted in the opposite seat, leaned back in the cushion, folded her arms over her chest, and as she did with Reba...arched a brow in anticipation.

Kate dug her fork through the mashed potato topping, took a bite, glanced at Allie wide-eyed, and smiled. "How did you get Mila to tell you the secrets to her spices?"

Allie shook her head. "Are you kidding me? I got an arm slapping, followed by a verbal assault, for even trying to guess."

"Then how did you—"

"Trial and error. I've been trying to recreate her magic touch since I came home. I know it's not the same and probably never will be, but I think I'm getting close. How is she, by the way?"

Kate stopped eating and leaned back in her seat.

"Kate? What's wrong?"

"Mila collapsed in the kitchen a couple of days ago. We flew her to Nassau for tests. She had a stroke. Her left side is partially paralyzed."

The air in the room felt suffocating as Mila's face flashed in Allie's mind, and the feeling of fondness she had developed for her became front and center. "Is she going to be okay?"

"That's a bit of a loaded question. After all, we're talking about Mila. The good news is, she's going to live, but her doctors say she will be facing some challenges. Of course, Mila is insisting she'll be back cooking for the resort in no time, and she threatened me within an inch of my life if I even think about replacing her. But in the meantime, I'm on the hunt for a temporary chef until we can figure out what this looks like going forward."

"Mila's going to have a fit when she finds out someone's going to be in her kitchen."

"I know, that's why I haven't told her yet. I'm sparing the hospital from her blowback."

Allie nodded her understanding. But the thought of Mila no longer being able to cook for the resort was something she knew would be like an arrow in her heart. "Wow, I'm really shocked and sorry to hear that. No one will be able to replace her, you know?"

"No. No one could ever replace her, she's one in a million. But I know a few chefs here in town who might be able to fill in for a while, until we figure it all out. Things won't be the same, and it'll be a hard adjustment for her, but when is change ever easy?"

Allie glanced at Kate and empathized with the pain she saw in her eyes. She instinctively reached for her hand, and the moment her fingers grazed over Kate's, every justification she had for remaining distant in the name of self-preservation was shattered. She leaned forward across the table and wanted, no needed, to feel Kate's lips on hers. To see if the deep connection to her that she had been so desperately trying to break free from was still there. She needed to hear the unspoken words between them. She licked her lips, closed her eyes, leaned in and…

"Allie!" Her mom's screeching voice was like an alarm clock waking her from a beautiful dream. "I need you over here, please."

"I um." Allie blinked as she stopped her motion. Holy shit, what was she doing? Recrossing this line was just going to set her back. And where would that leave her once Kate returned home? *No, don't go there Allie.* This road would only end in another heartache, and that was a path she promised herself never to venture down again. "That's my mom. I, uh, I should go." She scurried away from the booth and the grip of emotions that willed her to finish what she'd started. "Please, stay and finish your meal," she said over her shoulder as an afterthought.

"I'm staying at my parent's beach house in Malibu. Dad's in London, and Mom's on a safari in Africa. You're welcome to come by and stargaze tonight," Kate called.

Allie froze, closed her eyes, and let out a shaky breath.

"There's a telescope in the master bedroom," Kate added.

Damnit, those words hit her like foreplay. Kate was definitely playing her best hand. Allie turned. "We close at nine. I need to clean up and get mom home and settle her in. I can't make any promises."

"I understand. I'll text you the address and gate code. I won't hold my breath, but it would be nice if you could make it."

Allie nodded, turned her back on Kate and the desire to run into her arms and finish the kiss they'd almost shared in Hollywood-style, but she tamped down those feelings as she hustled over to her mom.

"Yeah, Mom, what's up?" she asked even though she knew the answer. Charlie needed his to-go box.

"She's beautiful, that one." Her mom gave a nod toward Kate. "And she gave you roses? I like her already."

"There's nothing to like, Mom, she's just a friend." And maybe that was all Kate had ever wanted. A friend with benefits package for the times their paths crossed.

Her mom scoffed as she waved a dismissive hand. "She's why you've been moping around ever since you got back, isn't she?"

"Mom, she's just a friend."

"So you keep saying and don't give me that look." She wagged her finger. "And don't tell me things that aren't true. Now, go fix Charlie his food. I've been worried about him lately. He's not looking so good."

Allie had noticed it too. Something had shifted in him last week. As though the little light that still sparkled in his eyes was fading.

"Hey, Charlie." She grabbed his half-eaten plate. "Let me go bag that for you." She hustled back into the kitchen and shoveled heaping portions of broccoli casserole and extra cups of cheese sauce in a container. She took another moment to smooth down her clothes and run her hand through her hair in the hope that she could rejoin Kate at the booth after she took care of Charlie, but when she emerged from the kitchen, Kate was gone, and a crisp, hundred-dollar bill was tucked under her plate.

It was close to midnight when Allie found herself standing outside Kate's house, hand frozen inches from the front door while she engaged in another debate between her head and her heart. She knew the reason she was here had nothing to do with stargazing, and what she assumed would transpire between them this evening would make her never want to leave Kate's embrace.

And again, how would that work? They both had a life far away from the other, and Kate had mentioned more than once how she could never return to the town that had sucked the soul from her.

Allie white-knuckled her fist and inhaled a deep breath filled with anxiety and anticipation. She took another moment to glance around at the entrance of the house and was reminded of the disparity in their economic statuses. A status that shouldn't matter, and yet, it did. They said love transcended all barriers, and as romantic as that notion was, she knew it was mostly bullshit. Especially in a city that not only glorified status and beauty, it also set the standard for it. In this town, you either had it, or you didn't. And she didn't. And years of watching Reba hook up with some of the actresses that she worked with, only to be quickly replaced by *one of their own*, had hammered that sentiment in even more. People like she and Reba never seemed good enough for those on the other side of the tracks.

Allie exhaled, did a little boxer warm-up dance, and knocked. Maybe she should just lighten up and accept it for what it might have always been. An attraction between two people that had manifested into beautiful lovemaking. And maybe that was all it was meant to be, and she was overthinking this. A long-distance relationship was financially out of the question for her, and leaving her mom so she could live with Kate pulled at her obligations to the point where she took that possibility off the table as well. That didn't leave many options between them. But who said this had to end in a *happily ever after*? Maybe *happily for now* was good enough.

"I was beginning to wonder if you'd show up." Kate opened the door and waved her in. She was back to wearing board shorts and a faded T-shirt, and that put Allie at ease.

Allie stepped inside. "It's not like Malibu is right around the corner from where I live, and the PCH was down to one lane for construction in some parts." She did a three-sixty and took in her surroundings. The dark-colored wood floor and ceiling beams offset the white furniture and cabinets beautifully. The art was simple and tropical in theme, and the overall vibe was rich elegance with a sterile feel. It reminded her of the few fancy hotel lobbies she had been to. Where the decor seemed like it was there to be appreciated, not used. "Nice place," she said, then focused on the floor to ceiling glass doors, the middle two of which were open, allowing the ocean to fill the house with its salty aroma. The patio deck was lit with white accent lights, illuminating two lounge chairs surrounded by planters of foliage, making it the most enticing setting in the house.

"I was sitting outside having a glass of lemonade when you knocked. It's a beautiful night to just get lost in your thoughts." Kate leaned against the door.

"Yes, it is," Allie said as she glanced in the direction of the patio and thought of her tiny apartment that had no balcony. But in her neighborhood, what would be the point? Her view consisted of a cluster of other apartment complexes, and the serenade would not be of the hypnotic sounds of the ocean's waves but instead, a mix of people and traffic. She took a moment and inhaled the salty air. She had been five when her parents had first taken her to the beach, and as soon as she'd laid her eyes on the ocean, her soul had felt at home. Her mom had told her she'd cried the entire trip back to their house after they'd packed it up and left. Her dad had said it was testament to the strong call Allie had to her heritage. Her mom had said it was no more than a kid not wanting the fun of playing in the sand and water to end. Either way, the ocean soothed her soul. She filled her lungs again and closed her eyes, but this time, the familiar scent of patchouli caused her to smile.

"I've missed you." Kate's words were soft and quiet, yet wielded a force so great, it sent chills through Allie's body as her butterflies took flight.

She turned, knowing Kate was behind her, and as she glanced in her eyes, she wasn't sure if she saw confidence or uncertainty. If it was the latter of the two, then it was good to know she wasn't the only one feeling that emotion.

Kate eyes searched Allie's. "You're so beautiful, and I'm so sorry for what—"

"Shh." Allie gently placed her finger across Kate's lips, stilling her words. She had not come here for a recap of what had happened. The multiple messages she had received the past few weeks had done that. She was here because Kate's presence was a pull she couldn't resist. Tonight wasn't about getting the full apology she wanted or fulfilling her hopes of a future together. No, this evening was about satisfying a hunger that had churned inside her the moment she'd seen Kate step into the restaurant. The reality between them was multilayered, emotionally charged, and seemed impossible to navigate, but right now, did she have to? She was becoming tired of chasing a future that never seemed to manifest itself. For once, she just wanted to live in the moment and let that be good enough.

But another night of amazing sex was not going to negate the reality that the morning would bring. Her mind shifted to a laundry list of action items: she needed to be at the restaurant in a few short hours to begin prepping for the day's meals; she needed to make sure the staff had everything under control by ten, so she could break free and take her mom to a doctor's appointment; she needed to meet with a local coffee vendor she was thinking of switching to.

The pressure from Kate's lips refocused her mind on the only thing that needed tending to at the moment.

"Mmm," she moaned. Kate's lips were soft, and they moved on her as if asking permission to proceed. She answered with a long, passionate kiss, and as their tongues became reacquainted, Allie's body told her all she needed to know. It might not hold the answers to their future, but it did hold an answer to the moment.

"I want you." Kate moaned as she unzipped Allie's jeans, placing a hand in her underwear and rubbing her fingers through her wetness.

"Bedroom," Allie said as she leaned out of the kiss. It wasn't a question as much as a directive.

Kate clasped her hand as she led her down a short hallway and into a bedroom. Allie took a moment to look around the spacious, minimally decorated room that had devoted one entire wall to glass. Although she couldn't see the ocean through the darkness of the night, she envisioned what it must be like waking up to its view every day.

Kate stepped in front of her and slowly walked her backward to the bed and lowered her down. She crawled on top and straddled her. Allie raised her hand and gently placed it on Kate's cheek. Kate leaned into it and closed her eyes. It was a simple and subtle gesture, and it made her heart beat wildly. Never had she wanted someone as much as she wanted Kate right now. She wrapped a hand around Kate's neck and pulled her down. It was clear since Kate was in the dominant position that she would once again dictate the dance between them, but that didn't mean Allie couldn't kick things off.

"I want," she whispered as she brought Kate's lips to hers. "To feel you in me. Because right now, I'm so fucking turned on that I'm about to come from just your kiss."

Before Kate could even reply, Allie plunged her tongue into her mouth and took command of the kiss while giving the rest of herself completely over to Kate. Her breath caught when Kate pinched her nipples and softly rolled them. Allie closed her eyes and arched her back to relieve the dual sensation of both the pain and pleasure.

Kate turned over on her side, shrugged out of her clothes, then wrapped her fingers around the waist of Allie's jeans and began pulling them down her legs. Allie felt the sensation of goose bumps appear on every inch of skin that the fabric exposed, and her butterflies took another lap around her stomach when her pants folded over her feet and were discarded on the floor.

As Kate returned to her previous position, Allie moaned, "Fuck me," in a soft whisper, more to herself as an expression of the pleasure she felt from what she was feeling. If Kate took her words literally, well, that was the nice thing about a statement that held so many meanings.

As Kate leaned down and kissed her deeply, she cleared her mind and focused on her body. Her senses were on high alert. Every inch of her ached to feel Kate's hands touch, pinch, or penetrate her. Kate broke the kiss and slowly sucked and licked down Allie's neck. She tilted her head back, giving Kate access to as much skin as she wanted as heat flushed her body and melted her heart.

"Mmm." Kate's moan floated to her ears, causing her nipples to harden even more as she prepared for Kate to take them like she had her tongue. "Your breast's...are so...perfect," Kate said between sucking and biting her nipples.

Allie tried to reply. To form a coherent sentence that told Kate how she felt. How Kate's actions were making her body heated with desire, and how she wanted Kate to perform the same motion on her clit. But it was impossible to speak. Her brain was concentrating on other senses, touch being at the top of that list.

Kate raised up, slid off her, and sat on bent knees at her side. The slight protest forming on Allie's lips was silenced by Kate's one hand massaging her breast and the other tickling down to the moisture that was building between her legs. Allie closed her eyes as she felt the tips of Kate's fingers play for a moment in her wetness but never slide in. She exhaled an excited breath for what was about to come. She tightened her stomach muscles and stiffened a bit as she tried to control her desires. If Kate continued to tease her like that, she would come any second. But that was not what she wanted. What she wanted was those same fingers to stop skating around and slip inside and fill her. The moment she felt Kate's fingers at her entrance, she arched her back as the sensation of three fingers filled her.

"You good?"

She responded by pressing her body more deeply onto Kate's fingers and moving her hips at an accelerated rate. Kate took the cue and began matching her pace. Harder. Faster. She caught her breath when one nipple was pinched, and the words, "Yes, baby," emerged from between her heavy breaths. A layer of sweat formed on her skin, and every time Kate went deeper, Allie moaned louder. Her body was now rocking back and forth with each thrust, and she reached out to grip the sheets.

"You're so wet."

The words not only gave her a chill, they also lit the fuse to what she knew would be one hell of an orgasm. As the buildup began, she concentrated every thought molecule she had on the pleasure happening between her legs. She rocked faster... pressed harder...until...

She leaned forward and tightened her muscles as the throbbing took hold around Kate's fingers. A moment passed, then two. She let out a contented exhale and slowly opened her eyes. As the pulsing subsided, she glanced at Kate, and there was something primal in her look that Allie understood. She reached between Kate's legs. Kate responded by widening them as Allie took a moment to cover her fingers in the wetness before sliding two inside. Kate lowered her body on Allie's hand, rocked up and down, and controlled the pace of her own pleasure. Allie twisted her upper body enough to reach Kate's breasts and tickled and teased her rosy, erect nipples.

"Yes, baby," Allie whispered as she watched Kate's face contort. "Yes, baby," she repeated until she felt the explosion inside Kate release.

"That was..." Kate huffed as she slowed her motion. "Beautiful."

Allie smiled and pulled her fingers out gently. Kate flopped next to her with a thud. They were side by side on their backs, breathing heavily as the air cooled the sweat beading on their skin.

"You are the most beautiful woman I've ever known," Allie said as she rolled to one side, lifted onto her elbow, and stared at Kate as she trailed a finger around her abdomen.

Kate tilted her head as she gazed at Allie. "So where do we go from here?"

Allie took the moment to think about the weight of her question. "I don't know," she said in a soft voice. "Where do we go from here?" She kicked the question back. She knew as long as her mom was still alive, she would be tethered to the diner. She did not have Kate's freedom or money to make a long-distance relationship work. That wasn't to say they couldn't figure something out in the meantime, but because of the obvious, that rested more on Kate's shoulders than hers.

Kate wrapped her arms around Allie and pulled her close. She nestled her head on Kate's chest and listened to her heartbeat. "Think we can figure out a way to make it work?" Kate said as she ran her fingers up and down Allie's back.

"There's a solution to every problem," Allie whispered the words her mom had told her when she was a frustrated child learning to cook for the first time. "We'll figure it out." Even though she had no clue what that looked like, did it really matter right now? In a few short hours, reality would kick in, and they would be pulled back to opposite lives that needed tending to. And in the immediate future, those lives did not include each other. But there was another saying her mom had always told her, or maybe it was something she'd seen online. Either way, it held truth: love would always find a way.

And as Kate's breathing changed into the soft slow rhythm of sleep. Allie's heart was full of equal parts love and sadness. She didn't want to set herself up with hopes and dreams of a future with Kate. Since none of her wishes had ever come true, why should this one? A few tears released with that thought and trickled down her cheeks. As she brought her hand up to wipe the wetness from her face, Kate stirred and in the sleepiest of voices, said the three words that made Allie wonder, for the first time in her life, if dreams really did come true.

"I love you."

EPILOGUE

Eight Months Later

"Ahoy there."

"Ahoy." Allie caught the rope Olivia threw out to moor her boat. "Wow, you got her painted." The old, rust-colored fishing boat she'd once rented was now shiny white, with the colors of the rainbow flag thinly painted as trim around its sides.

"I figured since I'll be working here, I should make her look a little more presentable." Olivia shrugged a backpack on her one shoulder, grabbed a small suitcase, and jumped onto the dock.

"It's so nice to see you again," Allie gushed as she embraced Olivia.

"Thanks again for the referral. I owe you one," Olivia said in a soft voice.

"You owe me nothing." The moment Jo had confided that she was going to turn in her resignation so she could move to Canada and be with Linda, Allie had told Kate about Olivia. A week later, a job offer was on the table, and Olivia accepted before Kate even discussed salary, benefits, or perks.

Allie broke the hug and turned at the sound of approaching golf carts. Kate and Carla were heading up the dock. Gizmo was trotting beside them, loudly grunting her greeting.

"Welcome." Kate parked, hopped out, and extended her arm as Gizmo flanked her and began squealing. "I'm Kate Williams, and that's Carla." She tilted her head over her shoulder. "And the loudmouth here is Gizmo. Please say hi, or she'll feel offended."

Olivia bent and rubbed Gizzy's head. "Well, hey there, Gizmo. Nice to meet you."

"She thinks she runs the place and that rules don't apply to her, and while that's pretty much true, if she ever oversteps her boundaries, just let me know," Kate said.

"And if ever something of yours goes missing," Allie added, "trust me, she's the likely culprit."

"Gotcha." Olivia nodded.

"Now, then, what can we help you with?" Kate asked.

"Nothing. I've got it all right here." She referenced her luggage. "The rest of my stuff I shipped over, and it should be arriving Friday."

"Well, let's put what you've got in Carla's cart." Kate motioned as Olivia hoisted her suitcase onto the back of the golf cart and hopped in next to Carla. "She'll get you settled in and answer any questions. I'll swing by your cabin in a bit to see how you're doing."

As they drove off, Allie nestled into Kate's arms and kissed her. "Mmm," she moaned. "I don't think I'll ever get tired of feeling your lips on mine."

"Then, what do you say we go back to the house, and I put them on other areas of your body as well?" Kate kissed the words down Allie's neck.

"Hold that thought." Allie leaned back. "First, you go help settle Olivia in while I walk over and check on Mila and Mom."

"You drive a hard bargain. Okay, give me a few minutes, then I'll swing by the kitchen and pick you up. Then we can... you know." Kate arched a brow.

"I know that look." Allie wagged a playful finger at her. "And you're on."

"Okay. I'll see you in a few." Kate hopped in the cart. "Are you coming with me, Giz?"

Gizmo didn't budge as she remained by Allie's side.

Kate began driving away. "Guess Giz is going with you," she called over her shoulder.

"Guess so." Allie glanced down as Gizmo looked up. "Come on, girl, let's go check on the ladies."

The day after they'd made love in Kate's Malibu house, Kate had offered to move Allie and her mom to the cay, but her mom wouldn't hear of leaving the few longtime customers she had. So for the next four months, Kate had flown back to LA every other week to spend time with Allie. But after Charlie had died and her mom had received another notification informing them that their rent was being raised yet again, her mom finally did the unthinkable. She hung a closed sign on the diner's door for the first time since it had opened. Kate had made a deal with the restaurant across the street that she would cover the tabs of the remaining regular customers from Allie's diner so they wouldn't go without a daily meal.

One month later, Allie, her mom, and Little Warrior—a small black kitten Allie had found abandoned in a box by the restaurant's dumpster—moved in with Kate and Gizmo. That same week, Mila had returned to the resort. The stroke meant that she had to begrudgingly use a cane to help with the lack of stability on her left side. In her absence, Kate had her cabin redesigned to accommodate her special needs. Twenty-four hours later, their temporary chef had announced she was quitting after Mila had unleashed a mouthful of profanity and her wooden spoon on her. But since it had become abundantly clear Mila could no longer handle full-time cooking, Allie and her mom had stepped in.

Reluctantly at first, Mila had agreed. They'd worked out a system where Mila told them what to do, and they followed her orders to a T, never questioning a single ingredient or process of preparation. And to everyone's surprise, her mom and Mila hit it off. They openly complained about their ex-husbands, talked about a lifetime of struggles while running a food establishment, bitched about what the world had come to, and in the middle of their daily rants and grumbles, had formed a friendship.

"Hi, Mom." Allie entered the kitchen, grabbed an apron, leaned in, and kissed her mother on the cheek.

"Hi, sweetie," her mom said.

"Hi, Mila." Allie pecked Mila on the cheek as she adjusted the apron cord around her waist.

"What's you doing? Go on, get before I smack you." Mila wiped her cheek with the back of her hand, but not before Allie noticed the corners of her mouth twitch. "If I wanted a wet face, I'd go and get a kiss from that damn pig."

Gizmo grunted and bobbed her head up and down as Mila let out a playful snarl, reached over, scratched her on the head, and handed her an apple. "Go on, now, get." She shooed as Gizmo trotted out of the kitchen.

The day Mila had returned to the resort, Gizmo had stayed by her side for two solid days. Allie had interpreted it as Gizmo's happiness to see her again, but Mila had said it was Gizzy just wanting to annoy her. Yet, more than once, Allie had caught Mila limping from the kitchen back to her cabin with Gizmo by her side as she told her stories about the rehab center, how god-awful the food was, and how their chef should be fired.

For the next hour, the three of them worked in tandem as they prepared the meal for the night's dinner. This week, the resort was filled to capacity with a wedding party, and Allie couldn't help being caught up in the infectious mood the love brought to the island.

❖

By the time Kate arrived at Olivia's cabin, Carla was sitting in her golf cart out front scrolling on her phone.

"Hey." Kate pulled up next to her. "How's Olivia settling in?"

"Fine. I gave her the five-minute tour of the place, and now she's changing into her uniform. I figure she can shadow me for the day, then I'll hand her off to Patti to train for the remainder of the week."

"Good idea. I'd like to get her on the schedule as soon as—"

"Well," Olivia interrupted as she emerged from the cabin with outstretched arms. "How do I look?"

Kate glanced at the khaki shorts, navy blue polo shirt with the resort's logo, and matching baseball hat. "Like you're one of us."

"Hop on in, girl." Carla patted the seat next to her. "My phone's already blowing up with things that need tending to."

Kate watched Olivia scoot in next to Carla, and they were in full chatter by the time Carla pulled away.

"She seems nice," Brooke said as she appeared next to Kate.

"She does." Kate turned her cart in the opposite direction and headed to the kitchen. "I think she'll fit right in."

"And the place is really looking good."

"I think so too." Kate nodded as they wound down the path. "I had more flowers planted and patio lights strung for this week's wedding."

"It makes me happy to see so much love on the island. Everyone seems like they're having such a wonderful time."

Kate glanced over. "It's what you always wanted."

"It was only a part of what I wanted. Seeing you so happy and full of life was my biggest dream." Brooke placed a hand on Kate's cheek, as Kate tilted her head toward her shoulder. "I'm so glad you found Allie. She's made you smile again."

Kate beamed. "She has."

"Then give her what you once gave me and let my dream for you live on. Fly free, my love, and finish with her what we started. You're in love, so let the second half of your life's story begin."

"It already has." Kate said as she approached the kitchen and parked. "You know I'll always love you, Brooke."

"And I you. Now go be with the one who just caused your heart rate to jump a few beats."

Kate grinned, hopped out of the cart, and leaned against the kitchen's door frame. "How are my favorite women doing today?" Kate said as she removed her sunglasses.

Allie approached and kissed her.

"If you two are going to smooch, then get out of my kitchen." Mila shooed with her hands. "Got no time for that in here. Got to prepare dinner. So go on, get."

"But the rolls still—" Allie began to plead.

"But nothing. This here's still my kitchen, and if I tell you to get, then get. Your mother and I can handle things just fine. Been taking care of myself my whole life, so I don't need no whippersnapper like you telling me I can't." Mila grumbled as Allie's mom averted her eyes and smiled.

Allie held her hands up in surrender, removed her apron, and told her mom to call her if she needed anything. She wrapped an arm around Kate's waist as they strolled to the golf cart and hopped in.

As Kate followed the path to her house, she caught Allie glancing out at the ocean. She turned. The water sparkled as it danced with the sunlight, and she squinted her focus beyond the shore. "You see something out there, babe?"

"Oh, I was just thinking of dad." Allie's voice was soft.

Kate entwined her fingers with Allie and brought her hand to her lips. Kate had bought Allie a small dive boat as a welcoming gift, and once a week, Allie took her mom to the spot where she'd buried his urn so Allie's mom could say her hellos.

"You know," Allie continued. "It's kind of funny how my family's story, which had no truth or substance, led me to you."

"It was fate, my love."

"Maybe. Or maybe it's the universe finally answering one of my dreams."

"Oh yeah, which one is that?"

"The one where I wished for a beautiful woman and a fairy-tale romance ending." Allie leaned in and kissed Kate's cheek.

"And is that what you have?" Kate turned and raised a brow, and as she parked in front of her house, Gizmo came trotting over to greet them.

"I think it would be fair to say my life exceeds all I could have ever dreamed for," Allie said as she bent and scrubbed her fingers under Gizmo's chin.

"So does mine." Kate pulled Allie close and passionately kissed her. "Bedroom or patio?"

"Since we made love on the patio last night, let's do the bedroom."

Kate nodded, and as she led the way, she thought about her future. Life had dealt her an interesting hand, that was for sure. It gave as much as it took. And right now, even though Kate was enjoying her chosen family in all its shapes, sizes, and temperaments, she knew there would be more heartache down the road because that was just a fact of life. But unlike before, she knew this time, she would bounce back. Brooke had once told her the depth of one's hurt equaled that of their feelings. And right now, as she glided Allie onto the bed, she couldn't feel more in love.

About the Author

Toni Logan grew up in the Midwest but soon transplanted to the land of lizards and saguaro cactus. She enjoys sunset hikes, traveling, and spending time with family and friends. Toni also writes erotic romance as Piper Jordan.

Books Available from Bold Strokes Books

An Independent Woman by Kit Meredith. Alex and Rebecca's attraction won't stop smoldering, despite their reluctance to act on it and incompatible poly relationship styles. (978-1-63679-553-9)

Cherish by Kris Bryant. Josie and Olivia cherish the time spent together, but when the summer ends and their temporary romance melts into the real deal, reality gets complicated. (978-1-63679-567-6)

Cold Case Heat by Mary P. Burns. Sydney Hansen receives a threat in a very cold murder case that sends her to the police for help where she finds more than justice with Detective Gale Sterling. (978-1-63679-374-0)

Proximity by Jordan Meadows. Joan really likes Ellie, but being alone with her could turn deadly unless she can keep her dangerous powers under control. (978-1-63679-476-1)

Sweet Spot by Kimberly Cooper Griffin. Pro surfer Shia Turning will have to take a chance if she wants to find the sweet spot. (978-1-63679-418-1)

The Haunting of Oak Springs by Crin Claxton. Ghosts and the past haunt the supernatural detective in a race to save the lesbians of Oak Springs farm. (978-1-63679-432-7)

Transitory by J.M. Redmann. The cops blow it off as a customer surprised by what was under the dress, but PI Micky Knight knows they're wrong—she either makes it her case or lets a murderer go free to kill again. (978-1-63679-251-4)

Unexpectedly Yours by Toni Logan. A private resort on a tropical island, a feisty old chief, and a kleptomaniac pet pig bring Suzanne and Allie together for unexpected love. (978-1-63679-160-9)

Bones of Boothbay Harbor by Michelle Larkin. Small-town police chief Frankie Stone and FBI Special Agent Eve Huxley must set aside their differences and combine their skills to find a killer after a burial site is discovered in Boothbay Harbor, Maine. (978-1-63679-267-5)

Crush by Ana Hartnett Reichardt. Josie Sanchez worked for years for the opportunity to create her own wine label, and nothing will stand in her way. Not even Mac, the owner's annoyingly beautiful niece Josie's forced to hire as her harvest intern. (978-1-63679-330-6)

Decadence by Ronica Black, Renee Roman, and Piper Jordan. You are cordially invited to Decadence, Las Vegas's most talked about invitation-only Masquerade Ball. Come for the entertainment and stay for the erotic indulgence. We guarantee it'll be a party that lives up to its name. (978-1-63679-361-0)

Gimmicks and Glamour by Lauren Melissa Ellzey. Ashly has learned to hide her Sight, but as she speeds toward high school graduation she must protect the classmates she claims to hate from an evil that no one else sees. (978-1-63679-401-3)

Heart of Stone by Sam Ledel. Princess Keeva Glantor meets Maeve, a gorgon forced to live alone thanks to a decades-old lie, and together the two women battle forces they formerly thought to be good in the hopes of leading lives they can finally call their own. (978-1-63679-407-5)

Murder at the Oasis by David S. Pederson. Palm trees, sunshine, and murder await Mason Adler and his friend Walter as they travel from Phoenix to Palm Springs for what was supposed to be a relaxing vacation but ends up being a trip of mystery and intrigue. (978-1-63679-416-7)

Peaches and Cream by Georgia Beers. Adley Purcell is living her dreams owning Get the Scoop ice cream shop until national dessert chain Sweet Heaven opens less than two blocks away and Adley has to compete with the far too heavenly Sabrina James. (978-1-63679-412-9)

The Only Fish in the Sea by Angie Williams. Will love overcome years of bitter rivalry for the daughters of two crab fishing families in this queer modern-day spin on Romeo and Juliet? (978-1-63679-444-0)

Wildflower by Cathleen Collins. When a plane crash leaves eleven-year-old Lily Andrews stranded in the vast wilderness of Arkansas, will she be able to overcome the odds and make it back to civilization and the one person who holds the key to her future? (978-1-63679-621-5)

Witch Finder by Sheri Lewis Wohl. Tamsin, the Keeper of the Book of Darkness, is in terrible danger, and as a Witch Finder, Morrigan must protect her and the secrets she guards even if it costs Morrigan her life. (978-1-63679-335-1)

A Second Chance at Life by Genevieve McCluer. Vampires Dinah and Rachel reconnect, but a string of vampire killings begin and evidence seems to be pointing at Dinah. They must prove her innocence while finding out if the two of them are still compatible after all these years. (978-1-63679-459-4)

Digging for Heaven by Jenna Jarvis. Litz lives for dragons. Kella lives to kill them. The last thing they expect is to find each other attractive. (978-1-63679-453-2)

Forever's Promise by Missouri Vaun. Wesley Holden migrated west disguised as a man for the hope of a better life and with no designs to take a wife, but Charlotte Rose has other ideas. (978-1-63679-221-7)

Here For You by D. Jackson Leigh. A horse trainer must make a difficult business decision that could save her father's ranch from foreclosure but destroy her chance to win the heart of a feisty barrel racer vying for a spot in the National Rodeo Finals. (978-1-63679-299-6)

I Do, I Don't by Joy Argento. Creator of the romance algorithm, Nicole Hart doesn't expect to be starring in her own reality TV dating show, and falling for the show's executive producer Annie Jackson could ruin everything. (978-1-63679-420-4)

It's All in the Details by Dena Blake. Makeup artist Lane Donnelly and wedding planner Helen Trent can't stand each other, but they must set aside their differences to ensure Darcy gets the wedding of her dreams, and make a few of their own dreams come true. (978-1-63679-430-3)

Marigold by Melissa Brayden. Marigold Lavender vows to take down Alexis Wakefield, the harsh food critic who blasts her younger sister's restaurant. If only she wasn't as sexy as she is mean. (978-1-63679-436-5)

The Town that Built Us by Jesse J. Thoma. When her father dies, Grace Cook returns to her hometown and tries to avoid Bonnie Whitlock, the woman who pulverized her heart, only to discover her father's estate has been left to them jointly. (978-1-63679-439-6)

A Degree to Die For by Karis Walsh. A murder at the University of Washington's Classics Department brings Professor Antigone Weston and Sergeant Adriana Kent together—first as opposing forces, and then allies as they fight together to protect their campus from a killer. (978-1-63679-365-8)

A Talent Within by Suzanne Lenoir. Evelyne, born into nobility, and Annika, a peasant girl with a deadly secret, struggle to change their destinies in Valmora, a medieval world controlled by religion, magic, and men. (978-1-63679-423-5)

Finders Keepers by Radclyffe. Roman Ashcroft's past, it seems, is not so easily forgotten when fate brings her and Tally Dewilde together—along with an attraction neither welcomes. (978-1-63679-428-0)

Homeland by Kristin Keppler and Allisa Bahney. Dani and Kate have finally found themselves on the same side of the war, but a new threat from the inside jeopardizes the future of the wasteland. (978-1-63679-405-1)

Just One Dance by Jenny Frame. Will Taylor Spark and her new business to make dating special—the Regency Romance Club—bring sparkle back to Jaq Bailey's lonely world? (978-1-63679-457-0)

On My Way There by Jaycie Morrison. As Max traverses the open road, her journey of impossible love, loss, and courage mirrors her voyage of self-discovery leading to the ultimate question: If she can't have the woman of her dreams, will the woman of real life be enough? (978-1-63679-392-4)

Transitioning Home by Heather K O'Malley. An injured soldier realizes they need to transition to really heal. (978-1-63679-424-2)

Truly Enough by JJ Hale. Chasing the spark of creativity may ignite a burning romance or send a friendship up in flames. (978-1-63679-442-6)

Vintage and Vogue by Kelly and Tana Fireside. When tech whiz Sena Abrigo marches into small-town Owen Station, she turns librarian Hazel Butler's life upside down in the most wonderful of ways, setting off an explosive series of events, threatening their chance at love…and their very lives. (978-1-63679-448-8)